PRAISE FOR WALTER DEAN MYERS

"Walter Dean Myers was . . . a visionary."
—Jacqueline Woodson, National Book Award–winning author
of *Brown Girl Dreaming*

"He wrote about disenfranchised black kids, particularly boys . . .
with extraordinary honesty and also with compassion.
Besides his books, his legacy is his compassionate identity with
these young people."
—Avi, Newbery Medal–winning author of
Crispin: The Cross of Lead

"[Walter Dean Myers] wrote with heart and he spoke to teens in a
language they understood. For these reasons, and more, his work
will live on for a long, long time."
—Susan Katz, former president and publisher of
HarperCollins Children's Books

"With vast literary talent and deep empathy for young readers,
Walter Dean Myers created shelves full of books over the course of
his half-century career that were groundbreaking, distinctive,
and vital."
— Andrew Medlar, Children's Literature Legacy Award
Committee Chair

"Students have told me that if not for Myers's books,
they would not read."
—Jessica Fenster-Sparber, library coordinator,
Passages Academy

"Fast, wry, and honest . . . the search for personal identity is at the
heart of this lyrical collection, and so is the sense of place."
—*Booklist*, Boxed Review

"Myers grapples with complex moral questions that will definitely
make readers stop and think."
—*Booklist* on *Monster*

"Enduring truths, winningly presented."
—*Publishers Weekly* on *Slam!*

"Sober, thought-provoking, rich in insight and detail:
another splendid achievement."
—*Kirkus Reviews* on *Somewhere in the Darkness*

ALSO BY WALTER DEAN MYERS

On a Clear Day

Hoops (based on an original screenplay by John Ballard)

Darnell Rock Reporting

Me, Mop, and the Moondance Kid

The Outside Shot

What They Found

145TH STREET

SHORT STORIES

WALTER DEAN MYERS

DELACORTE PRESS

Text copyright © 2000 by Walter Dean Myers
Jacket and map art copyright © 2020 by Kgabo Mametja
"Harlem: Then and Now" copyright © 2020 by Penguin Random House LLC
"Celebrating Walter Dean Myers" compilation copyright © 2020 by Penguin Random House LLC
Tribute by Rudine Sims Bishop copyright © 2020 by Rudine Sims Bishop. Tribute by Pauletta
Brown Bracy copyright © 2020 by Pauletta Brown Bracy. Tribute by Michael Cart copyright ©
2020 by Michael Cart. Tribute by Natasha Díaz copyright © 2020 by Natasha Díaz. Tribute by
Cicely Lewis copyright © 2020 by Cicely Lewis. Tribute by Lois Lowry copyright © 2020 by Lois
Lowry. Tribute by Dr. Claudette S. McLinn copyright © 2020 by Claudette S. McLinn. Tribute by
Christopher Myers copyright © 2019 by Christopher Myers. Tribute by Jason Reynolds copyright
© 2020 by Jason Reynolds. Tribute by Nic Stone copyright © 2020 by Logo Lepsy Media Inc.
Tribute by Deborah Taylor copyright © 2020 by Deborah Taylor. Tribute by Renée Watson
copyright © 2020 by Renée Watson.

All rights reserved. Published in the United States by Delacorte Press, an imprint of Random
House Children's Books, a division of Penguin Random House LLC, New York. Originally
published in hardcover and in slightly different form by Delacorte Press,
an imprint of Random House Children's Books,
a division of Penguin Random House LLC, New York, in 2000.

Delacorte Press is a registered trademark and the colophon
is a trademark of Penguin Random House LLC.

Grateful acknowledgment is made to Malin Fezehai for permission to reprint the top left
endpaper photograph, used by permission of Malin Fezehai, all rights reserved,
and to the Walter Dean Myers Estate for permission to reprint all remaining endpaper
photographs, used by permission of the Walter Dean Myers Estate, all rights reserved.
With special thanks to Christa Angelios, Colleen Fellingham, Regina Flath,
Alexandra Hightower, Kamal Nassif, and Ericka O'Rourke.

Visit us on the Web! GetUnderlined.com
Educators and librarians, for a variety of teaching tools,
visit us at RHTeachersLibrarians.com

Library of Congress Cataloging-in-Publication Data
Names: Myers, Walter Dean, author.
Title: 145th street : short stories / Walter Dean Myers.
Other titles: One Hundred Forty-Fifth Street
Description: First edition. | New York : Delacorte Press, [2020] | Originally published: New York :
Delacorte Press, 2000. | Summary: Ten stories portray life on a block in Harlem.
Identifiers: LCCN 2019018311 (print) | LCCN 2019021633 (ebook) | ISBN 978-0-385-72984-0 (el) |
ISBN 978-0-593-11966-2 (hc) | ISBN 978-0-385-90538-1 (glb)
Subjects: LCSH: Short stories, American. | CYAC: African Americans—Fiction. | Harlem (New
York, N.Y.)—Fiction. | New York (N.Y.)—Fiction. | Short stories.
Classification: LCC PZ7.M992 (ebook) | LCC PZ7.M992 Aae 2020 (print) | DDC [Fic]—dc23

ISBN 978-0-593-11966-2 (20th Anniversary Edition)

The text of this book is set in 12-point Minion.
Interior design by Blake Morgan and Ericka O'Rourke.
Printed in the United States of America
10 9 8 7 6 5 4 3 2 1

Random House Children's Books supports the First Amendment
and celebrates the right to read.

*To Beryl Banfield,
for her contributions to
multicultural literature*

CONTENTS

BONUS CONTENT

145th Street
Celia's House
JACKIE ROBINSON MEMORIAL PARK
BIG JOE'S HOUSE
BIG JOE'S BBQ & BURGER RESTAURANT
EEZ-ON-IN CAFÉ
UNITY FUNERAL HOME
MISS PAT'S HOUSE
FREDERICK DOUGLASS BOULEVARD
GRACE TABERNACLE CHURCH
DUKE'S BARBERSHOP
RALPH J. BUNCHE SCHOOL
MALCOLM X BOULEVARD
ADAM CLAYTON POWELL JR. BOULEVARD
Harlem

Big Joe's Funeral

The way I see it, things happen on 145th Street that don't happen anywhere else in the world. I'm not saying that 145th is weird or anything like that, but it's, like, intense. So when I heard about Big Joe's funeral it didn't take me by surprise. It was something that I remember, and that's why I'm telling it. This is the way it went down.

The funeral took place on the Fourth of July, one of the hottest days of the year. People were sitting out on their fire escapes or on their front stoops trying to catch a breeze. If there was a breeze in the 'hood it must have stopped somewhere for an iced tea because I didn't see or feel it. Nobody was doing any unnecessary movements unless their name was Peaches Jones, who was setting out to ruin Big Joe's funeral.

Peaches was what you would call seriously fine. She

was fifteen, about five feet three, a medium brown color, and definitely wrong. She was wrong because she was not giving Big Joe his propers, which means his proper respect. A person ought to have respect for other people all of the time, but especially at two times during their life. The first time is when they are born. When a baby is born you shouldn't say discouraging things about it like "Hey, I seen prettier dogs than that baby," or "Maybe he ain't ugly, maybe he's just inside out." Give the baby a chance.

The other time you need to show some respect is when a person is going on out of this world. You know, like they're dead and whatnot. Let the person go. Whatever will be their reward has got to be figured out on the other side. Even if they slip on out owing you some money, you got to bite the bullet, give up some slack, and let them be on their way. But Peaches didn't see it that way when it came to Big Joe. She had her mind dead set on messing up Big Joe's funeral.

Let me back up here and tell you: It all started when Big Joe, who owns Big Joe's Bar-B-Que and Burger Restaurant, right here on 145th Street down from the Eez-On-In Cafe, decided to cancel his life insurance. He said he had been paying on his life insurance for twenty years. If he canceled his insurance he would get a check from the insurance company for eighteen thousand dollars. Now, that is some serious money. It sounded good when the guys in the barbershop were talking about it. So Big Joe canceled his insurance and sure enough, two weeks later, he was telling everybody that the check came just like he thought it would. That's when he decided to have the funeral.

"I have always loved a good funeral," Big Joe said. He was sitting outside his restaurant, peeling potatoes to make potato salad. "And when I went to Freddy's funeral—y'all remember Freddy?"

"Yeah, I remember Freddy and his funeral," Willie Murphy said. "He looked real good."

"That's my point," Big Joe said. "He was looking better than I have ever seen him. He was clean, had his hair combed, and wore that dark suit with a carnation in his lapel."

"He was sharp!" Willie went on. "And when Angela, that little Puerto Rican girl, sang 'Precious Lord,' everybody was crying."

"Ain't nobody was going to cry over Freddy when he was alive," Big Joe said. "Funerals bring out the best in people. Am I lying or flying?"

"You definitely flying," I said.

"I hate to talk about the dead," Willie added, "but when Freddy was a walkie-talkie all he wanted to do was to hang out on the corner and ask everybody he seen if they had any spare change so he could take it down to the Eez-On-In and get him a beer."

"Un-huh, but he still had him a nice funeral," Big Joe said. "I'm going to have me a nice funeral while I'm still alive so I can appreciate it."

Now, we didn't exactly know what Big Joe meant by that but when he started explaining, it made sense. He was going to take part of that eighteen thousand dollars and throw himself a funeral the way some people throw a party.

"Nothing too fancy," he said. "Just something nice."

Now, this is what he did. He went over to the Unity Funeral Home on Adam Clayton Powell Boulevard and arranged things with them. At first Old Man Turner, who ran the place, was a little put out, but then he saw where live people having funerals would greatly increase his business and he said okay. He was going to supply the coffin, the hearse, which carried the coffin, and two limousines. The good part of this is that since I was there when Big Joe was first talking about his funeral I was going to get to ride in one of the limousines.

Big Joe asked Leroy Brown, who had a little band, to play the music at his funeral. Then he found Angela, that little girl who had sung at Freddy's funeral, and asked her to sing a song.

Now, you're probably wondering what Sadie, Big Joe's girlfriend, thought about all this. Well, she didn't like it one bit.

"You don't mess with dying," she said, her hands on her hips. "You go laying up in some coffin and death liable to reach out and snatch you right away from here!"

"Woman, you're just superstitious," Big Joe said. "Ain't nothing to worry about."

Sadie was a widow lady, her husband having been run over by an ambulance while he was on the way across Malcolm X Boulevard to buy a Lotto ticket. Maybe her being a widow was what made her touchy. But if she was a little upset it was nothing compared to what her daughter, Peaches, felt. When Peaches heard about Big Joe's plans she was madder than a junkyard dog with fleas.

"He's been asking my mama to marry him for the last year," Peaches said. "If he's going to be a good husband what's he doing going around acting stupid?"

"Is she going to marry him?" I asked.

"She doesn't need to marry him or anybody else," Peaches said.

Big Joe had promised Sadie he was going to adopt Peaches once they were married. That looked like a good deal to me because Big Joe was really successful and everybody liked him. Not only that but the brother was handsome, too. He was tall and dark and had white hair at the temples, which made him distinguished-looking. Peaches and her mama argued up one side of Big Joe and down the other but he didn't change his mind. He was going to have his funeral.

Big Joe was popular on 145th Street. If you were a little down on your luck and needed a meal, or a pair of shoes, or even half the month's rent, you could go to Big Joe and he'd listen to you and more than likely help you out, too. So by the day of the funeral it looked like there was going to be a big turnout.

Now, besides Sadie and Peaches there were some sisters from the church who thought the idea was a little peculiar and they made sure that everybody knew it, but even some of them showed up because they appreciated a good funeral, too.

Well, the Fourth of July was hot but the undertaker's

parlor was air-conditioned. There were only two funerals scheduled for that day, Big Joe's in the afternoon and a funeral for somebody named Calderone later that night.

When we came into the funeral parlor there was Big Joe, lying up front in his casket. It spooked me out. Big Joe wasn't moving a muscle and you could see he had on some of that makeup they put on dead people. Sadie was sitting in the front row with her arms folded and her jaws tight.

When it was my turn to file past the coffin I did so real slow. I knew that Big Joe was alive but I didn't know what I would do if he suddenly sat up. I was glad to sit back down again.

The funeral director's wife played some songs on the organ and then Angela sang her heart out; there were real tears running down her face. Then some of Joe's friends stood up and said good things about him.

Leroy's band, the All Star Stompers, played "Amazing Grace" and "One More River to Cross" and before you knew it we were deep into the funeral. I looked over at Sadie and she was getting a little misty, too.

When the inside part of the funeral was over the undertaker shut the coffin. I watched to see if Big Joe was going to move. The dude didn't even twitch.

When we got outside, the hearse and the limousines were waiting, and so was Peaches. She and two of her friends, LaToya and Squeezie, had painted these big signs. They read, BIG JOE IS NOT DEAD.

Mother Fletcher, who might be the oldest woman on the block, was just passing by and saw them. She went over to them. I went over, too, because I wanted to know what she was going to say.

"You're right, child," Mother Fletcher said. "The flesh fades but the spirit lives on to its eternal reward!"

"That's not what I mean," Peaches said. "I mean he's really not dead!"

"Suffer the little children!" Mother Fletcher said as she started walking away. "Glory, hallelujah!"

Peaches and her crew held up their signs across the street and people on the block looked at them and looked at the funeral and most of them didn't know exactly what was going on. Chops Peterson came over to me and said, "Peaches should mind her business."

"If Big Joe is supposed to be her daddy someday, maybe it is her business," I said.

"He's not her daddy yet," Chops said.

By then they had loaded Big Joe into the hearse and the rest of us got into the limousines and we started up to Jackie Robinson Memorial Park.

Jackie Robinson Memorial Park was a playground on one side, and on the other side were just benches and a few trees. We were going to pick out a spot in the park and have a ceremony there like it was really a grave.

"I want to hear some dirt falling on the casket," Big Joe had said.

Now, to me that was going a little too far. I didn't think I could lie in no casket, even if it was cracked some so I could breathe, and hear dirt being tossed on it. I was glad it wasn't me in there.

I might have split right then, but I knew the last part of the funeral was going to be okay. After the ceremony we were all supposed to leave feeling good. Leroy's band would play some jazz and the whole thing was going to turn into a party that would end up in Big Joe's place.

When we were pulling away from the funeral parlor I saw Peaches and her girls taking down their signs. I figured they knew they had lost the fight. We were going over toward Malcolm X but they were headed in the opposite direction in a big hurry.

First the cars went down to 141st Street, where Big Joe lived, and we went past his house real slow, showing respect to where he had spent his life, then we turned and went up to 145th and past the restaurant real slow. Some brothers playing checkers on the corner took their hats off when we went by. Then we went up the hill to the park.

When we got there the undertakers pulled out the coffin and put it on a roller and rolled it right onto the grass. That's when I saw Peaches and her crew again. They waited until we reached the place where Mr. Turner, the undertaker, had set up a little shade tent. Then they turned on the boom box they were carrying, and blasted a song called "I'll Be Glad When You're Dead, You Rascal You!" all over the park.

Peaches had the boom box right up close and it was going as loud as she could get it going. LaToya was dancing and people heard all the commotion and started gathering around. They were looking at each other and trying to figure out what was going on. There was this girl dancing to this old-time song and a funeral going on right in the middle of the park.

Two winos drifted over to see what they could see

and a bunch of kids stopped playing and gathered around.

"Yo, brother, y'all going to bury somebody right here?"

I turned around and saw this short dude carrying a hot dog in one hand and a book in the other. He tilted his head down and looked over his glasses at me.

"We're not really going to bury him," I whispered. "We're just going to throw some dirt on him before the party starts."

The brother took a giant step back from me and shook his head. "You *are* crazy, right?"

I just shrugged.

Right about then I thought the whole thing was going to come to a quick close because I saw two cops coming over.

"What you mean I got to move on?"

"You better get your hands off me!"

This is what Peaches and Squeezie were saying to the cops.

"It's against the law to have your boom boxes turned up like that," one cop said. "And you should have more respect for a funeral."

Now I could see the cops eyeing us and looking at the coffin and one of them was talking on his radio. They weren't sure if what we were doing was right, but they knew what to do about a loud boom box. So they took the box, and Peaches, LaToya, and Squeezie went after them.

Leroy's band broke into "Swing Low, Sweet Chariot" and then they lowered the coffin onto the ground and threw a couple of clumps of dirt onto it up near the top so Big Joe could hear it. The funeral was officially over. The undertaker reached down and knocked on the wood to let Big Joe know. For a while nothing happened and I held my breath. All eyes were glued to the coffin. Then it popped open and Big Joe sat up. People who didn't know what was going on moved back in a big hurry and one of the winos took off running.

Big Joe got out of the coffin and shook everybody's hand.

"Let the party begin!" he said.

Leroy's band broke into a reggae number and we started bopping on out the park.

We piled back into the cars and headed on down to Big Joe's place with the horns going and people waving out the windows.

When we reached Big Joe's you could smell the food cooking. Big Joe's cousin Ernie was handing out sodas and we started going into the restaurant. That's when we heard the sirens. Now, sirens on 145th Street are no big deal. They got dogs on the street that have heard the sirens so many times they can imitate them perfectly. But when the police cars all pulled up in front of Big Joe's and the cops came out with their guns drawn we knew something serious was going on.

"Freeze!" A big, puffy-looking cop pointed a gun right at Leroy.

Leroy froze and so did I.

In a minute they had everybody lying on the ground.

"Where's the dope?" a policeman kept yelling. "Where is it? Where is it?"

"What's going on?" Big Joe yelled from where he was lying, next to the fire hydrant.

"We got a call that somebody was bringing in a shipment of crack in a coffin," the policeman said. "Where is it? Where is it?"

Willie pointed toward the hearse and the cops surrounded it. About that time I saw Chops get up and sneak away.

"I got my rights." Leroy was lying facedown.

"Shut up, Leroy," one cop said. We all knew the cop, O'Brien, and he knew most of us, but we didn't like him and he didn't like us. "If we find narcotics you're all going to jail."

They searched the coffin, the hearse, all of us, and two guys who were just sitting on their stoop, but they didn't find anything because naturally there wasn't anything to find. Then one of the officers received a message on the radio and got real excited.

"Wrong coffin," he said. "We just got a tip!"

Then the cops took off without even telling us to get up. Everybody was mad but in a few minutes the partying was on and we forgot about the police. When Chops showed up he called me over to one side.

"Me and Peaches," he said.

"You and Peaches what?" I said.

"I figured Peaches made the first call," he said. "I made the second call telling the cops that the drugs were in another coffin."

"Chops, you are something else," I said.

He just grinned.

We all had a great time at Big Joe's party. Everybody

made stupid jokes about how good he looked for just coming from his funeral, and how he shouldn't eat too many ribs because it was bad for his cholesterol.

"It could kill you," Willie said.

There was some talk about the cops making us lie down on the ground. Big Joe was mad about that, but the party lifted everybody out of their bad mood. I ate some more ribs, some fried chicken, and a mess of potato salad. Some folks got into an argument about whether the Fourth of July was a better holiday than Memorial Day, and they really enjoyed that, too. It was the best holiday I had had since Christmas and just about the best party.

I went on home and told my moms about the funeral and the party and she said it was okay if Big Joe wanted to waste his money but if she had any extra money she would have bought a new sofa.

About three-thirty the next morning I heard sirens again and I looked out the window and saw that there were two police cars and an ambulance down in the street. I thought the police were looking for that crack they had heard about, but later in the day I heard that Cassie, who lives on the third floor, had called them because her husband was beating on her. They took him away and their two little girls were in the street crying.

That's what 145th Street is like. Something funny happens, like Big Joe's funeral, and then something bad happens. It's almost as if the block is reminding itself that life is hard, and you have to take it seriously.

The word on the street was that Cassie went to Big Joe and got the cash she needed to get her husband out of jail. Cassie probably wasn't going to pay him back the money and Big Joe knew it, but he lent it to her anyway.

"And the next time I have a funeral," Big Joe said, "I better hear you there crying and carrying on."

Cassie smiled and went on up 145th Street toward the subway.

The Baddest Dog in Harlem

We were all sitting around on the rail outside of Big Joe's place, trying to figure out which was the best fighter of all time. We'd had this conversation before but what got everybody mad this time was Willie Murphy. Willie was in his thirties, or maybe even older, and was the kind of guy who thought that just because he was old it meant he knew more than anybody.

"You have to go with Joe Louis being the best fighter of all time," Willie said. "Joe held the championship for longer than anybody."

"That's because he didn't have to face Ali," Tommy said.

"How about Roberto Duran?" Pedro was sitting on a folding chair that was chained to the gate that covered Big Joe's place.

"Duran's not a heavyweight," Willie said. "When

you talk about the greatest fighter of all time you have to talk about heavyweights."

"Why?" That's what I said.

"Because you do," Willie answered.

Now, that was a lame answer and everybody there, with the exception of Willie, knew it.

The conversation was getting to be stupid and I knew it was going to get worse, because Mr. Lynch was coming down the street. Mr. Lynch was so old he had washed dishes at the Last Supper. Whatever you said he would bring up something from a thousand years ago that nobody ever heard about.

"What you young people talking about?" Mr. Lynch motioned for Pedro to get off the chair.

"These know-nothing kids thinking Ali could've taken Joe Louis." Willie started flapping his lips again. "Ali couldn't have taken Joe Louis if Joe was fighting with a paper bag over his head."

"Ain't none of them could beat Jack Johnson," Mr. Lynch said, parking his old butt on the chair. "Jack Johnson was the champion of the world and he fought all over the world."

"Ali would have eat him up," Willie went on. "Now, that's one thing I know."

Just when I was heated up enough to go upside Willie's head we heard this squealing on the corner and we looked up and saw two police cars come tearing around the corner. They pulled up right in front of us and the cops come out with their guns out. Now, I wasn't a fool and I knew when the police come tearing like that they're looking for somebody. I did just like everybody else leaning on that rail did, said a quick prayer and put on my innocent face.

One of the cops came over to us. "How long you guys been here?"

"Two hours, maybe three hours," Pedro said. "Except for Mr. Lynch. He just got here."

The cop took a glance at Mr. Lynch. Then he went over to Willie and started patting him down.

Willie just stood there and I hoped he didn't have anything on him illegal. Then the cop asked him how long he had been there and Willie told him the same as Pedro did, except for Mr. Lynch, we had all been there about two hours.

Then I saw an officer pointing to one of the buildings and when he did that all the cops got around behind their cars and started crouching down as if they were expecting some heavy shooting.

"Hey, we're gonna move on down the street," Tommy called out to the cops.

"You stay right where you are!" this big cop called out, and like he meant it, too.

Then the next thing we did was to look up at the building to see if we could spot anybody shooting. Now, I figured if there was a crazy dude up there shooting at people he was liable to shoot at us instead of whoever he was mad at.

"Hey, man, we sitting ducks here on this rail," Willie said. "And I'm sitting here on the end."

"You're lucky," I said. "If it is some crazy fool he's

liable to be aiming at you and hit one of us. Least if he hits you first it'll give us a chance to duck."

"Hey, Mr. Officer," Pedro called out, "we got to get away from here 'fore we get shot up."

The cop looked over at us and didn't say nothing. I bet if he had his way he would have had us sitting out there in that police car.

Some more cop cars came and before you turned around there's about seven cars and a whole mess of people milling around 145th Street, trying to figure out what was going on. Then the kids started coming around and everybody was looking up at the windows where the cops were looking.

One thing about 145th Street. Half the guys on the block don't have jobs and so they're always on the stoops or just standing around with nothing to do. And after a while that gets boring, so when the cops arrive like this it breaks the day up nice. Unless it's you they're looking for, of course.

"Junior! Junior!" Old Mrs. Davis come running out of the Laundromat with her fat self. "Junior! Junior!"

"Get back, there . . . !"

Things were getting out of hand and the police tried to get people to move across the street. One of them got on the bullhorn and told all the kids to get off the street immediately. He must have meant that as a joke. The kids didn't have anything to do and they weren't going anyplace.

So you had the kids just standing there looking at the cops and then you had Mrs. Davis moaning and going on about where Junior was. Junior is a wino who does little odd jobs around the block, but anytime any trouble goes down his mama starts running around screaming for him like he's four or five years old.

"There's somebody up there!" a kid yelled.

Now, what did he say that out for? Everybody hit the ground, including me, and covered up the best they could.

I hadn't seen anything, but then I wasn't looking too hard. The thing I don't want to be is a witness.

Once I got on the ground I figured I was gonna stay on the ground until the mess was over with. But then I saw Willie sliding on his belly down the way and into the Eez-On-In, the little soul food place. I went right behind him and soon we all on the floor of the restaurant.

"What's going on?" Mamie, the girl who worked there asked, when all these guys came crawling into the restaurant.

"The cops are looking for somebody," I said. "You better get on down here on the floor next to me so I can protect you."

Flood, the manager, was eating a sandwich and he just slid down to the floor and kept on eating. Right then a policeman came in and told everybody to get down. He was crouching and the rest of us were down on the floor on our bellies and he was telling us to get down.

"What's going on out there?" Mamie asked.

"We got a report of a man with an automatic weapon," this cop said. "Anybody here know anything about it?"

We all said no and then the cop eased out.

"What they mean about some automatic weapon?" Pedro asked.

"It means when it hits your butt you're automatically dead," Mamie said, and she got a good laugh out of that.

That laugh that Mamie got lasted about a good ten seconds when all of a sudden we heard another one of them big-eyed kids saying something about seeing somebody at a window.

We stuck our heads up a little so we could see what was going on. One of the cops started running around the front of the car and slipped on some dog doo. When he hit the ground his gun went off and a shot came through the window of the restaurant. There was glass all over the floor and Willie let out a scream. By this time the cops were shooting away at that window.

They must have shot maybe a hundred shots and people was running and screaming. One cop went down behind a car and when Mamie looked she said he was bleeding.

"They got him in the head!" she called out.

The mess was getting serious. Willie was bleeding right next to me and now the cop was shot in the head. I slid over to the counter and started to get behind it.

"We don't allow nobody behind the counter," Flood said. "You know that!"

Outside the shooting started again and I squinched under the counter the best I could. Mamie got down next to me and I put my arm around her and she snuggled up.

After a while the shooting stopped and I heard somebody outside say, "They got the guy with the automatic weapon and it was some Arab!"

We waited for a while and then started getting up from the floor. I stayed behind the counter in case it broke out again. Then we all kind of edged around outside to see what we could see. I looked around. No cops had been shot, but the guy who had slipped in the dog doo was having his elbow looked at. We heard somebody shout and everybody hit the ground again. But then we saw that it was just Mary Brown. Mary is one of those smart sisters who has a good job downtown.

She pointed up to the window that the cops had shot out.

"You shot up my new drapes! I don't work all day for you fools to be up here shooting up my drapes!"

"Who lives in that apartment with you?" this cop with some gold braid on his hat said.

"Nobody!" Mary say.

"Where's your boyfriend?" the cop asked.

"I don't know where he is," Mary said. "But wherever he is, he's not messing up my new drapes!"

"If he's up there they just killed him," somebody said.

"Let's go, lady," this cop said. Then he went to take Mary by the arm.

She snatched it away from him and said she wasn't going anywhere with them unless she had a black man with her. She started looking around for somebody to go with her when a cop grabbed me by the arm and said, "You come with us."

"Hey, why I got to go?" I asked. "I don't know anything and I don't want to see no dead people."

Didn't do a bit of good because they made me go up there with them. My knees were shaking and I had to pee so bad I didn't know what to do. Mary was going up the stairs like she was in a hurry to get somewhere. The cops made us go up first and they came behind. I tried to turn around and they gave me a push in the small of the back but I saw they had their guns out and they were looking more tense with every step. They had one cop who was a brother but he was trailing behind and looked like he was fixing to run any minute.

When we got to the floor where Mary lived I held my breath and closed my eyes. If I was going to die I sure didn't want to see it coming.

Mary went to her door and started fishing out her keys and the cops stood on either side of the door. She unlocked the door and then the cops eased me and her back. Then they hit the door and rushed in.

What I saw when they let me in was something I will never forget as long as I live. There was about a couple thousand bullet holes all over the room. The ceiling was all shot up from where the cops had been shooting from the street. The window was all shot up. Her drapes were raggedy. The refrigerator was shot up. The stove was shot up. The kitchen cabinet was shot up. She had a box of salt that was so shot up it was all over the room. But that wasn't the worst part of it. Right in the middle of the floor was her dog, deader than a doornail. I don't know how he could've got himself so shot up like that. They must've hit him once and then he didn't know what to do with himself and kept trying to get back in front of the window.

"You killed my dog?" Mary put her hands over her face and let out a long wail. "You killed my dog?"

Mary sat on the side of the bed that wasn't covered with plaster and began to cry. The cops just looked for a while and then they started getting themselves together.

"That dog look like a terrorist to me," one of them said. You could see they were breathing easy again.

"That's probably the baddest dog in Harlem." That's what the cop who was a brother said.

"How are we going to write this up?" one cop asked. He had got there after everybody else but you could tell he was a boss.

"I know one thing," Mary said, "somebody's going to pay me for this, and that's the truth. I'm going to sue the city."

We all felt a little better about things then and I was glad I was the one that went up with Mary so I could tell the others. We were just at the top of the stairs fixing to go down again, when the first cop stopped quick and I looked to see what he was looking at. He was standing a few feet from a door at the end of the hall. It was open just a little. The cops looked at each other and the guns came out again.

The routine was the same as Mary's place. They called out for anybody that was in there to come out. When nobody came out two cops wearing bulletproof vests rushed the door. Five or six cops went in behind the first two and there was some shouting inside and then nothing. Then, one by one, the cops came out.

Their faces were pale. Something was wrong big-time. They whispered something to the officer in charge and he nodded. Some of the cops started downstairs with Mary. One stayed behind and leaned against the wall. I pointed toward the door, and the cop shrugged. I went to the apartment and pushed the door open.

It was a one-room place like Mary had. It wasn't shot up near as bad as her place. A few bullet holes here and there, a catsup bottle busted up on the floor. Then I looked at the bed and saw the kid.

He was a little knotty-headed boy with lips that stuck out like he was pouting, and skinny black legs that twisted oddly away from his body. The television was on with the sound turned down. The way I seen it, the boy was home watching cartoons when he heard all the noise outside. Then he must have turned down the TV and went to the window to see what was happening.

I didn't see where he was hit, but I saw all the blood on the bed and it didn't take a whole lot of figuring to see he wasn't breathing. A feeling came over me, like I was lying on a beach at the edge of a lost world with a wave of hurt washing over my body. I looked at that kid's face again. He could have been my little brother or cousin and I wanted to say something to him, but I knew it wouldn't do any good. I covered him up, went on outside, and closed the door behind me.

The cops took Mary downtown to make some kind of statement and I went on down to the street. I knew what I wanted was to hear Pedro and Willie and Tommy and all the other brothers and sisters on the block talking about that kid. I wanted them to say how bad they felt about it and what a shame it was the way life could slip away so easily in Harlem, in our community, on our street. Maybe when we got together and let our pain out it would rise up and reach someplace where the kid could feel it, too. I don't know if any of that made sense, but it was how I felt.

"Is it true what they said about shooting a dog?" Willie asked.

He took my arm and looked into my face. I didn't have to tell him there was more to it.

Fighter

Billy Giles told his wife that he was just going to the gym to work out. If he'd told her the truth, that he was going to fight again, he knew she would have cried.

"You're not going to eat anything?" she asked.

"No, I'm not hungry," he said. He had seen her making supper, and had known that he wouldn't be eating anything.

"Don't stay out too late," she said. She reached up and touched the tip of his nose with her index finger. "I'll think you're out with another girl."

"I'll bring you some ice cream," he said, framed in the doorway of their apartment. From where he stood he could see into the bedroom where the baby's crib stood against the wall.

He closed the door, waited for a moment for the click that said that Johnnie Mae had locked it, and started down the stairs. He felt a little sick to his stomach. There had been a time, not too long ago, when he would have been excited to be boxing. Somewhere between that time, between sixteen and nineteen, the nervousness had turned to a kind of nausea that he would dream about in the early hours of the morning.

Chops and Tommy were on the stoop talking to some girl he didn't know. The air was cool and he sucked it in between his clenched teeth. The smell of fried fish was heavy in the air and he wished that he had eaten something.

He started the long walk up the hill toward the Eighth Avenue subway. Win or lose he'd take a cab home. Now he walked slowly. There wasn't any hurry. It was seven and he wasn't scheduled to fight until ten. It would take less than a half hour to get to the Bronx gym and minutes to get into his gear.

On the corner a guy played a saxophone, the sound sliding into the darkness and echoing off the bricks. It was too cold to be out playing a saxophone but Billy guessed the guy was dealing with demons that needed to hear a tune. You did what you had to do, he thought.

The program hadn't started when he reached the gym and made his way to the fighters' entrance. There was a bunch of girls hanging around on the first floor, and Manny was in the middle of them. Manny flashed him the high sign and he flashed back. He went upstairs where Al Gaines was listening to the radio.

"Get out your clothes and I'll tape your hands," Al said. "Manny talk to you?"

"No," Billy answered.

"He said he might want to put you on early," Al said.

"It doesn't make any difference to me," Billy said. He took off his street clothes as Al tried to find a better station on the little radio he had been bringing to the gym since Billy knew him. Billy put on his groin protector and slipped into the green trunks he always wore.

Al kept up a steady stream of talk as he taped Billy's hands. Billy grunted his answers and tried to think about the first time he had fought for Manny. Manny had worked his corner that night, had kept yelling at him to "show strong," and he had won. After that first professional fight he remembered walking out into the night, his face still stinging from the blows he had received, and feeling taller than he had ever thought possible.

Al finished with the taping and Billy shadowboxed in front of a mirror. Other boxers were in the locker room; some were changing clothes, others listened to music. A young, awkward kid was bragging about how he was going to start the night off by knocking out his opponent. Billy knew he was afraid.

The room was too small for all the nervous sweat, for all the odors, for all the heat that the bodies generated. Now he sat on the end of the rubdown table, smoothing the edge of the tape with his forefinger as if it were necessary, listening for sounds that would tell him the fight in progress was over and that it was his turn. He had been fighting preliminaries for nearly three years and knew his limitations and abilities. He would win or lose tonight—it made little difference. Either way he'd collect the one hundred and forty-five dollars for the bout. If he put up a good show there'd be another preliminary bout for him when a spot became available. He could pay some bills and still have enough to take John-nie Mae to a movie.

A fighter he knew, Jimmy Walls, was warming up in the corner. Billy watched him for a while; his black skin already glistened with crystals of sweat as he threw deft combinations against an imaginary, helpless opponent. It was an odd thing with Billy: He could never imagine, even when he shadowboxed, an opponent he could easily beat.

Billy heard a strong buzz from the crowd outside and knew that something had happened. Probably a knock-down or a knockout, he thought; maybe the brash kid had made good his boast. Billy's stomach tightened and he took deep breaths. He'd been knocked down in the last fight but had won on points. And after, when he'd gone home, Johnnie Mae made tea for him and offered it as he sat wearily in the faded, overstuffed chair they had somehow inherited from his married sister. When he reached for the tea he missed the cup, and Johnnie Mae had panicked.

"What's wrong, baby, what's wrong? You hurt?" She put the cup down on the table, tipping it over, ignoring it in her concern.

"Nothing wrong. I'm just tired," Billy said as the moment of dizziness passed over.

"You're not fighting anymore, Billy, you hear that? You're not fighting anymore, that's final now!" Johnnie Mae stood twisting a dish towel, letting her voice rise almost to a scream.

"You want to wake the baby?" he countered.

Billy knew that the money he was able to pick up in the ring meant more to him than to his wife. Being a man meant saying yes when your woman asked you for something. She didn't understand that, at least she didn't understand how it made him feel when he heard her making plans and dreaming about things that cost money he didn't have.

It was good, too, to complain about not being made of money but then to reach down and give her enough cash to have her hair done or get something for the baby. Later, when the baby was a little older, maybe they'd get a baby-sitter and Johnnie Mae could work for a while until they were doing better. Then he would give up fighting.

The door to the dressing room opened, startling Billy. The two fighters came in. It was easy to tell who the winner was.

"Hey, Billy, what's happening?"

The winner. The kid who had bragged about getting a knockout skulked to a corner, slipped out of his trunks, and fumbled with the lacing on his groin protector, the grease still on his eyebrow where he'd been cut. The fighter who had beaten him said he'd put up a good fight, said it loud enough for the loser to hear, as they always did. Billy felt sorry for the loser, knowing that at that moment he felt beaten and ashamed and hated the boxing he'd hoped would bring him to glory.

"Let's go, Billy." Manny Givens managed about six fighters, all of them fighting in minor fights, only a few of them still hoping for the big time. "Guy's a comer, kid, watch him."

Billy started the trek to the ring. This was the only good part of the fight—the crowd looking at him, wondering what he was made of, judging him by his swagger, by the expression on his face, his show of confidence. Unconsciously he tried to impress them as he walked to the ring, as if they were his adversary and not the other fighter. Manny guided him with pats on the back. Then he was in the ring. The other fighter was already there, a young Puerto Rican, close to his age.

Manny had said the guy was a comer. In Manny's ring talk it meant that the guy was being groomed, that he had been carefully brought along and given only fights he was expected to win. In the office, when they planned the fights and decided what the money would be, the Puerto Rican would be considered the "fighter" and Billy would be the "opponent." The Puerto Rican's name was Danny Vegas.

"Okay, boys, you know the game, keep up the pace." The referee had finished the introductions and called them to the center of the room. The heat was unbearable. "I don't want to have to tell you to fight. Give the folks a show. Touch gloves now."

Billy touched gloves and went back to his corner.

"If you get him," Manny said, rubbing Billy's shoulders, "there could be some breaks involved." He didn't sound convincing.

The bell rang.

Billy came to the center of the ring and snapped a glove out. It was a quick move and hit Vegas on the forehead. Crouching low for a minute and then quickly straightening, he faked Vegas out of position and banged his hands to the wiry body. They backed off and circled each other cautiously. Billy told himself that he would win, that he could take this guy. He threw jabs, feeling Vegas out, checking out his moves. Vegas, for his part, seemed not too anxious to mix it up with him and they spent most of the first round fighting at a distance.

Sitting in his corner always made Billy think of commercials being played on television between the rounds. His trainer gave him a swig of seltzer, which he spit into the bucket. He'd been shocked, after his first fight, to discover that he was expected to pay for even the seltzer he used between rounds.

In the second round, Billy found out why Manny had called Vegas a comer. They were in close, shoulder to shoulder, and Billy was again throwing punishing hits to the body, hearing Vegas grunt from the force of the blows. Billy could have continued fighting on the inside while he had the advantage but elected instead to back away for more power. He had, for a moment, an image of himself, fists flashing, rendering Vegas helpless against the ropes. Billy backed off, feinted once, jabbed, feinted again, twice, disregarded completely a right thrown by Vegas as he prepared a series of blows to the body and head.

He didn't see the blow coming and it stunned him. There was a sudden lack of focus and a scary awareness of his knees. Billy pushed off and bobbed and weaved. Vegas didn't know that he'd been hurt, and when Billy managed to throw a light jab it was Vegas who grabbed and held on. Then they were apart again and Vegas was snapping his glove in Billy's face. Billy thought he was cut.

The glare from the overhead lights gave Vegas's face an unreal appearance. Billy felt almost as if he were fighting a thing rather than a man. Vegas would try a move and Billy would know what he was going to do, but he couldn't stop it. He could see the confidence in his opponent's face.

Now he was against the ropes with Vegas punching him in the body, jolting nausea into him in sharply swelling waves. Billy was having trouble keeping his mouthpiece in. For a moment Vegas dropped his hands and with a frenzy Billy lashed out at him, more in fury than with any plan.

There were noises from the crowd as Vegas backed across the ring. Billy was surprised to find himself following, throwing punches. They were apart again, circling one another, when suddenly Vegas turned and went to his corner. Billy hadn't heard the bell ring but walked back to his own corner.

"Maybe you could go to school. Take IBM or something." Johnnie Mae *sat on the bed, pushing the baby back into the middle whenever she crawled near the edge.* "It would be hard but you have to make sacrifices."

Some people could do it. When Billy thought of them he always pictured young guys with glasses and attaché cases sitting primly on the A train and thumbing through a thick book. He had told Johnnie Mae that he'd finished high school, but he really hadn't.

And now that she had made such a big deal of it, he

couldn't tell her. School. Billy remembered standing in the back of the room at Junior High School 271, not being allowed to sit down until he had brought his mother in to see the teacher.

"What are you wasting your time for?" the guidance counselor had asked him. "You think it's going to be easy out there?"

That was the last day Billy had gone to school. Not that his mother wouldn't have taken the day off from the button factory where she worked to come down, but because it seemed true, that he was wasting his time. Learning for him had always been hard, like catching water in his bare hands, it would all slip through, all be so near and yet somehow not useful to him. If only they'd talked about things that he knew something about.

"The rounds are even," Manny said. "Start fast."

Vegas hadn't been expecting it and was momentarily stunned when Billy threw a high right to his head.

Billy followed it with a left hook, leaving his feet for a moment, seeing the force of the blow contort Vegas's face. Vegas slumped to the floor. The referee was counting over him.

"One . . . two . . . three . . . four . . . five . . . six . . ." Vegas was on one knee at six and on his feet at eight. Billy moved in fast. Vegas moved away, slid along the ropes, picked off a wild left that Billy threw, and missed a jab himself. He tried to clinch and Billy pushed him away with one hand and swung for his head with the other. He missed and Vegas threw a right hand that caught Billy just in front of the ear.

His vision doubled. He was in trouble. From every angle there seemed to be someone throwing punches. Billy's mouthpiece had fallen to the canvas and the referee kicked it toward his corner. He tried desperately to keep his hands up. Pride would keep him in the fight.

In the appliance store, when the clerk had asked if he was interested in the nineteen-inch screen Billy had said no, he wanted the thirty-two-inch screen.

"That's a good choice," the clerk had said. "It's a good buy at seven hundred dollars."

Later he would have to tell Johnnie Mae that he had changed his mind, that the thirty-two-inch set was too big for their small living room, but for the moment, in the store, he couldn't back out of the game.

Billy couldn't tell for sure where Vegas was, only that he himself was being hit. Barely conscious, he spread his hands, knowing he was going down. Still Vegas smashed his fists into his face. He heard the cheering of the crowd as he fell. Above him a brilliant confusion of lights glared down. There in the middle of the arena, in the middle of the ring, in the middle of the light, the referee standing over him, he felt like he always knew he would feel, alone.

Then, somehow, he was up, and Manny was forcing the acrid smelling salts under his nose, forcing him back to reality. He knew he must have been knocked out. Manny asked him something and he felt that he had slurred the answer, but Manny seemed satisfied.

Vegas was lifting his arm, saying that he had fought a

good fight. The special policemen were coming into the ring for the next fight. They told Manny to have Billy leave from the corner without stairs and he had to jump from the ring.

Billy didn't stop to pack his gear neatly, just crammed it into his bag. He showered slowly, surprised to find out how sore he was in the body. Later there would be blood in his urine. Later there would be the headaches that kept him up in the early mornings. He had been knocked out before. He knew what he would feel like in the morning and told himself that it didn't matter.

He got the money from Manny.

"Billy, give me a call in a month or so." Manny looked away from him. "When you get yourself together."

At the gate he had to wait until a special policeman opened it so he could leave the arena. Behind him the crowd was noisy, cheering. It had started to rain. Billy decided to take the subway home. He didn't deserve a cab. On alternate stations he tried to figure out what he had done wrong against Vegas and then what he had done wrong in life that had him in a half-empty train trying not to throw up.

He remembered his promise to pick up some ice cream for Johnnie Mae, but the grocery store on the corner was closed and he didn't feel like walking down to 142nd Street to the one that was open.

Johnnie Mae was awake. When she saw him she knew that he'd been fighting and that he'd lost. She didn't say anything, just helped him undress.

Outside, the rain picked up and now beat hard against the window. From down the street a tinny-sounding radio oozed out a slow blues. Johnnie Mae was crying, but she didn't say anything. Billy took the money out of his pocket and threw it on the table. Johnnie Mae picked it up and threw it on the floor. Then, realizing that she had hurt him, picked it up and put it carefully back onto the dresser.

Johnnie Mae wiped the traces of alum from his face with a wet, cool cloth. It should have been left on, but he let her do it anyway.

"I love you, baby," she said. "I love you so much."

Later Billy, lying in the darkness, listened to the even sounds of his wife's breathing. He wondered if somewhere in the city Vegas was lying in bed dreaming about fighting, about their fight. Billy checked the time; it was a little after two. He found Johnnie Mae's hand and held it. Even in her sleep she took his hand and squeezed it gently. He needed that squeeze, that gentleness, the knowing that the gentleness would always be there, that through all the nights of pain to come, she would be there for him. He closed his eyes and hoped he wouldn't dream.

Angela's Eyes

The wind, whistling across the vacant lots and through the redbrick and fire escape canyons of the neighborhood, had taken another summer. Old men brought out their faded suit jackets and moved their domino games inside. Theresa, the mother of Angela Luz Colón, finally emerged from her grief and called the factory where she had worked before her husband, Fernando, had been killed. They told her she could come back to work, and she did.

That is not to say that she had stopped crying against the wall at night or stopped reaching out her hand in the darkness to where he had lain by her side for so many years. It was just that she had also begun to rise, once she had watched the gray mist of twilight give way to early sun, and leave for work.

"You should go out more, too," she told her daughter. "Remember what the priest said about putting aside sorrow."

She left out the part about rejoicing that another soul had found peace in the Lord.

Angela did go out more. She went to her seventh-grade classes, to the store, sometimes for walks alone in the park. These things she did when it was time for them to be done. She still spent a lot of time thinking of her father. The thoughts often came to her as she sat alone in the kitchen waiting for her mother to come home in the evenings. She would think of his laugh, the way his brown face would wrinkle around the eyes and the wide smile would fill their small kitchen. On weekends he would rise early, shower, and prepare breakfast for Angela and her mother. The comforting sounds of ham frying would announce that he was ready for them to come to the table even before he knocked on her door.

Then the dreams began.

It was Poli, the old man that worked in Mr. Rodriguez's bodega, that Angela first dreamt about. She dreamt that she was at school when suddenly her father walked into her classroom. Then it was not her father who stood before the class, but Poli, stoop-shouldered beneath his white hair. His sad, dark eyes seeming to look into her very soul. Angela felt the same sadness for him that she had felt for her father. Later, when she went into the bodega to buy olive oil, she saw Poli sorting tomatoes in the window. She stood, not thinking, looking at him until her eyes misted with tears.

"Hey, Angela, what's wrong?" Mr. Rodriguez came over to her. "How can such a pretty girl be sad?"

"It's nothing," Angela said.

"It's got to be something," Mr. Rodriguez said.

Angela told him of her dream. Poli and another woman came over and listened, both nodding their heads as Angela spoke. The woman said that the dream was sad, but Mr. Rodriguez and Poli looked up the dream in the Black Cat dream book to see which number to play. Dreaming about a school was 3-5-6, which was also Poli's house number. Then they came up with 2-3-7, which was Angela's house number, and since her father had recently died, they played 0-6-5, for death.

Poli played the numbers the next day and then forgot them. Mr. Rodriguez played them all that week. None of them came out, but Poli died.

"He called and said that he didn't feel well," Poli's grandson said. "He had a pain in his shoulder. The hospital said he had a heart attack."

The Sunday after Poli's funeral the domino players drank rum and talked about him, about how good he was and about the old days in Mayagüez when Poli had raised pigs until his first wife left him and he had come to the United States. They talked about Angela, too. About how her dream had predicted his death. Mr. Rodriguez said that sometimes children see things. Jorge Cruz, who was older than Mr. Rodriguez and whose face was lined with his years, said that when a man dies violently he leaves his eyes to his child, and that it was her father, looking from the other side of darkness, that had seen Poli's dying. Not much was said after that but it had been enough to dampen the thin sound of the portable radio they had been playing.

What Jorge Cruz had said spread quickly around the neighborhood and soon everyone was saying that Angela had her father's eyes. When it came to Angela she went quickly home and looked in the bathroom mirror. She pushed her hair away from her face and looked into her own eyes. Some boys said that her eyes were pretty. To Angela they were too dark, like deep, bottomless pools.

When Mrs. Flores came into Mr. Rodriguez's bodega she said that it was strange that Angela had predicted Poli's death. This she said more to Maria Pincay and Titi Sanchez, who had come to buy plantains, than to Mr. Rodriguez, who she knew liked Angela very much and who looked with soft eyes on the girl's mother as well.

"Poli was an old man," Mr. Rodriguez said. "His time had come, that's all. Besides, when is death a stranger in this neighborhood? You can't pick up *El Diario* without reading that someone has died."

"Yes, that is right," Mrs. Flores said, crossing herself, "but how many times do you pick up a paper and see that some healthy person is going to die, eh? Tell me that."

"I tell you that you talk foolishly, woman," Mr. Rodriguez said. "The girl knew Poli, maybe she saw that he didn't look so good."

This was true, Angela had known Poli for many years. Mr. Rodriguez was pleased with the logic of his remark and noted that, although Maria Pincay did say that Angela had always been a little strange, it was a weakly offered statement.

But Angela had not known Eddie Robinson. He was the man who worked in the West Indian restaurant on 147th Street. He seemed a distant man, often lost in his own thoughts as he stood behind the counter stacking porgies in the basket for deep-frying. A dark, stocky man with sloping shoulders and large hands, he would scoop up a large portion of the breading mixture in one hand and, taking the fish in the other, would slap it from hand to hand until it was perfectly breaded on both sides. Then he would sprinkle the breaded fish with basil and stack it with the others. Angela had seen him do this but had not spoken to him about it or anything else. In truth, if it had not been for Mrs. Flores no one might even have known that Angela had ever seen Eddie Robinson.

"How are you doing?" Mrs. Flores asked when they met in the bodega. "I haven't seen you at Mass for a while."

"I go to early Mass with my mother now," Angela said.

"I saw your mother the other day and she looks good." Mrs. Flores had selected two cans of kidney beans and put them on the counter. "You must be taking good care of her."

"I try," Angela said, pleased with the comment.

"Have you had any more of your dreams?" Mrs. Flores asked.

Mr. Rodriguez looked up from where he was sitting with Jorge Cruz, a dark scowl crossing his face.

43

"Sometimes I dream," Angela said.

There were images in her mind. An image of Poli sitting in the park watching the children play basketball. An image of the funeral cars pulling away from the church, gliding away into the gently falling snowflakes.

"Who do you dream about?" Mrs. Flores asked, pretending to examine the label on a can of soup as the dark looks of Mr. Rodriguez burned into her back.

"My father, mostly," Angela replied.

"Angela came for eggs, not to talk about her dreams." Mr. Rodriguez got up from the card table and put his arm around the slim girl.

"Did you dream about me?" Mrs. Flores stepped to one side so that she could see Angela's face.

"No," Angela said, "I dreamt about the black man who works in the restaurant near the post office. Him and my father."

It stopped them. Mrs. Flores, Mr. Rodriguez, and Jorge Cruz. Even the moment stopped for the space of a heartbeat.

"She dreams about a place to eat," Mr. Rodriguez said finally, and twisted his face into a silly grin. "That's a good sign for a young girl, isn't it?"

Angela took the eggs and a package of sausages and paid for them. Jorge Cruz played idly with the cards as Mr. Rodriguez bagged Angela's purchases. When Angela had left, Mr. Rodriguez slapped the flat of his hand hard against the countertop.

"Why do you have to do this?" Mr. Rodriguez lifted his voice, a thing that was rare with him. "Why can't you leave the girl alone? We have bad girls in this neighborhood and you don't say a thing about them. This is a good girl, so why don't you leave her alone?"

"Lips speak lies, but the face speaks the heart," Mrs. Flores said, shaking a finger toward Mr. Rodriguez. "Jorge, did you see Mr. Rodriguez's face when the girl said that she dreamt of Eddie?"

"Who is this Eddie?" Mr. Rodriguez asked.

"You know, the black man who works in the little diner that the Greek used to have," Jorge Cruz asked.

"Yeah, I see him at the market."

"You won't be seeing him at the market much longer," Mrs. Flores said.

"I don't believe a word of it," Mr. Rodriguez said. "You're making something of nothing."

"What do you think, Jorge?" Mrs. Flores asked. "She has her father's eyes, no?"

"I don't know," Jorge Cruz said. "Maybe she has a special vision."

"What vision?" Mr. Rodriguez threw his hands up. "This Eddie is still alive, isn't he? If he dies it's you who puts the mouth on him, not her."

Eddie Robinson was born in Athens, Georgia, on the same day that Franklin Delano Roosevelt was first inaugurated. Eddie's father would have named him Franklin if he hadn't promised his cousin when the boy's mother was first pregnant that he would name the child after him.

So it was Eddie, and not Franklin, Robinson who was hit by a truck on Thanksgiving morning. Someone who saw it said that he had pulled up his coat collar and was leaning into the bitterly cold wind and never saw the truck coming. Others said that it didn't matter, that all that mattered was that Angela had dreamt of him, and that he was dead.

Surprisingly, it was Titi Sanchez and not Mrs. Flores who started the most trouble for Angela. This despite the fact that it was Mrs. Flores who spread it around the neighborhood that Angela had dreamt of Eddie Robinson. When Eddie died it was the same Mrs. Flores who went on with her did-you-hear's and her I-told-you-so's.

But when Mr. Rodriguez gave a party for his friends and best customers on the Wednesday before Christmas, which he had been doing for the ten years he had been in business, it was Titi Sanchez who piled the biggest burden onto Angela.

Perhaps it was the wine, or the heat from the kerosene burner used to supplement the cranky radiator, or perhaps an unlucky combination of the two. Titi was standing against the wall, beneath the plastic Malta Fresca sign, when she found herself looking into someone's eyes. The someone, sitting at her mother's side at the round table, was Angela Luz Colón.

"Don't look at me!" Titi screamed at her.

Angela looked quickly away, shocked by Titi's sudden outburst. Then, compelled to see what kind of creature would scream at her so, she looked again, searching in her eyes for reasons for this violation of her sensibilities.

"Don't look at me!" Titi screamed again and buried her head in her hands.

All eyes turned away from Titi toward Angela, but as the girl looked back the heads turned away quickly.

"What is wrong? What is wrong?" Angela's mother's

voice was like the screeching of a gull. Her eyes darted first to her daughter, then to those around her. "What is wrong?"

"Titi has had too much celebration." Mr. Rodriguez separated himself from two old friends. "Here, open another bottle of wine and let's relax and enjoy ourselves."

The party went on, but the musical lilt of voices, the cymbal lightness of laughter, did not. Angela's name pulsed beneath the hushed conversations like a muted drum.

When Titi was finally calmed by Sadie Jones and her cousin she apologized to Mr. Rodriguez through her tears.

"I'm sorry," she said. "I just don't want to die."

Mr. Rodriguez didn't answer her, just patted her lightly on the shoulder and told her, "It's okay, Mami."

When Titi left the others began to leave, too. Soon it was just Mr. Rodriguez, Jorge Cruz, Angela, and her mother who remained behind in the gaily decorated bodega.

"I hear what they say." Angela's mother had her arm around her daughter. "It's a terrible thing to say. This is America, not some jungle. Why do they say things like that?"

"Today they talk about Angela and tomorrow they'll be talking about me," Mr. Rodriguez said. "Half the people in this neighborhood don't have jobs, all they have for entertainment is what they can make up."

But they did not stop talking about Angela. When Titi went around saying that she did not want Angela looking at her because then she might dream of her it brought a nodded agreement, if not an "amen" and a hastily made sign of the cross.

There were images in Angela's mind. When her father died she had lived with the terror of knowing that he had been killed in his taxi, and that they had found him slumped over the wheel, just as she had feared for so many nights, ever since he had started driving. When it had come she was asleep. Her mother woke her to give her the news and then left to go to the hospital. She had lain in the darkness of her room, her mind blank, her body numb. Had she fallen asleep? She must have. When she was sure of her surroundings she recalled an image of her father. Had it been real? Or was it, perhaps, only the echo of a thousand headlines that had already screamed their violence into the deepest corners of her soul? Later, as she leaned against the cracked porcelain sink, the tea already cold in her thin hands, her mother and aunt returned from the hospital, their tear-streaked faces bringing her the news that the images had indeed been real.

That people began to shun her was the worse part. The eyes turning away were like a knife to the heart. She began to stay away from school, from the park, even from the bodega, wrapping the images that came to her around her waking moments as one wraps a cape around the shoulders on a cold day.

There was the image of her father sitting at the table across from her, his body framed by the high kitchen window, his cap on the back of the chair near his shoulder.

"Dying is not the bad part," he had said. "The bad

part is when the death grows in us. When we know it's coming. Then you mourn for yourself even before you go. It's the knowing that is terrible. When I die I want to die by getting hit by a comet at Yankee Stadium during the World Series."

"Why Yankee Stadium?" her mother had asked.

"I don't want to die alone, either," he had said, buttering his toast.

Perhaps it would have ended with Angela and her mother pressing themselves like two funeral lilacs between the yellowed walls of their apartment, had not Mrs. Morales also told Consuela Ortiz that Angela had the power to see death coming. Consuela Ortiz was a woman of forty-seven who lived in the projects. She was older than her years and much given to ruminating about her health. Further, she had had a strange feeling in her right side ever since a man had pushed her into a railing as they scrambled for seats on the IRT line. The more she thought of it the more she thought that it might, after all, be a cancer. And so she asked Mrs. Morales if she would arrange a meeting between herself and the girl, Angela.

Mr. Rodriguez wanted nothing to do with it when Mrs. Morales approached him, but Jorge Cruz said that it would be a good idea.

"If she can't do this thing," Jorge Cruz said, gently tapping his curved and yellowed nails on the card table in Mr. Rodriguez's bodega, "then we will know that the deaths just happened and everybody will feel better for it. If she can, then we will know that it is a miracle of God."

Mrs. Morales was not sure if the miracle would be of God or Satan, but she held her tongue while Mr. Rodriguez thought about it.

"I'll see what I can do about it," Mr. Rodriguez said.

The idea didn't sit well with him, but neither did the notion that the girl was so sad now. So he spoke first to the mother, telling her just how he felt, and then, with her permission, he spoke to them both and convinced them of Jorge Cruz's logic. Still, when they all found themselves in his bodega the following Saturday evening, they were not easy.

Jamie Farrell, who sometimes delivered packages for Mr. Rodriguez, was there, as were Maria Pincay, Mrs. Morales, and a few of her choice friends to whom she owed favors.

"My name is Consuela Ortiz." The woman's hands were shaking as she spoke. "I have a pain here."

She touched her side, somewhat embarrassed to be revealing herself before so many people. Then she paused, not knowing what to say next, or how to frame the question that she wanted answered.

"I don't know what to say to you," Angela said. "I don't know about your pain."

There were tears in Angela's eyes and her mother took her hand.

"Do you have dreams?" Mrs. Morales asked.

"Dreams?" Angela looked up at Mrs. Morales.

"I don't mean about me," Mrs. Morales said quickly, "I mean about her!"

There were images in Angela's mind. Images of a

city, of people walking, working, some sitting in the sun on benches. Were they eating lunch?

"I dreamt there was a noise, an explosion. It was on a nice day. . . ."

There were images in her mind. A cloud that shaped itself into a funnel and a funnel that shaped itself into a tornado, and then a giant mushroom, and then a cloud that covered half the earth.

". . . Many people were hurt," Angela said, trying to shut away what she had seen in her dreams.

"Did you see me?" Consuela Ortiz took her other hand.

Angela looked into the woman's eyes and shook her head. No, she had not seen her.

As Consuela Ortiz looked around the room many things happened. First there were the tears of relief that came to her eyes. Then the loud cry that crouched in Mrs. Morales throat, ready to spring when she heard the expected news, died where it lay. Then there were smiles on other faces and, lastly, Jorge Cruz brought his years and wisdom to the event.

"Sometimes a child sees things," he said, "which are large things to a child. But when the child gets older it sees more important things. Angela is dreaming about a war. That's why so many people were killed."

"I bet my last dollar," Mr. Rodriguez said, "that there will be another war. Probably something in the Middle East."

"By the time you get to your last dollar we'll all be too old to think about war," Maria Pincay said.

Even though the bodega had not done well that month Mr. Rodriguez broke out the wine. It was not a time for celebration, but neither was it a time for despair.

Angela started coming back to the bodega again after that and Maria Pincay got Titi Sanchez to apologize to her for what had happened at the party.

When a proper amount of time had passed Mr. Rodriguez began speaking with Mrs. Colón. He spoke of loneliness, and how the sun, even in the barrio, seemed warmer when shared. The consequences of their conversations seemed scant but they both seemed pleased with the possibilities, which, in turn, pleased Angela.

But Angela's dreams did not leave her. Or, rather, the dream did not, for they were all the same now. There would be a city, people walking, working, sitting in the sun on benches. Were they eating lunch? And there was a terrible noise and a flame that turned itself into a funnel, and a funnel that turned itself into a tornado, and then a mushroom, and then a great cloud that covered nearly half the earth.

She would be in the dream, sometimes with her father, sometimes not, running from house to house, unable to find an unshattered mirror to hold the fragments of her terror.

But she did not speak of her dreams again and, after a while, neither did anyone else. It was a silent pact that she had made with the world: She would not speak of the dreams that caused such trembling in her bosom, and the world would not turn away from her. It was hard for her at first, but soon she learned to cry only in her bed and to muffle the sound with her pillow.

"Sometimes," Mr. Rodriguez said, cutting up chickens for his meat case, "things happen that hurt us deeply, and even though it's something we think we should hold on to it's usually better to let it go."

"You mean my dreams?" Angela asked.

Mr. Rodriguez, having meant her grief over her father's death, nodded all the same.

The Streak

Okay, so my name is Jamie, Jamie Farrell. Remember that, in case I get famous or something. My main man, my ace, the Jack who's got my back, is Froggy Williams. Froggy is definitely for real. Only thing is that he doesn't know scratch about ball.

"So you missed a shot," Froggy said. "Big deal."

"So we lost to Powell Academy," I said. "We're the only team uptown that has lost to Powell."

"So what happened?"

"The game was down to fifteen seconds and we're losing by a point," I said. "Tommy Smalls steals the ball and they all jump up into his face. Me, I see Tommy cop the pill and I'm running down the court. My man is trying to double-team Tommy and so I'm free as I want to be and standing under the basket."

"Tommy didn't see you?"

"No, he sees me, jumps up, and gets me the ball with like two seconds to go."

"Yeah?"

"Then I blow the layup," I said.

"Why you do that?" Froggy asked.

"How do I know?" I said. "I was free, I didn't rush it, I banked it soft off the backboard just like in practice, and it rolled around the rim and fell off!"

"So you want to go by my crib and listen to some jams?" Froggy asked.

"Man, the whole school is on my case for blowing the game to dumb old Powell Academy and you talking about listening to some jams," I said. "What am I going to listen to, the Death March?"

"Yo, just forget it ever happened," Froggy said. "Life goes on."

"No, it doesn't," I said. "That was the first thing that happened today. Then I go into the locker room and all the guys are giving me the evil eye because I blew the game, right?"

"Yeah?"

"So I try to finesse it off and I'm sitting there drinking a bottle of WonderAde, okay?" I said, thinking maybe I shouldn't even tell him.

"WonderAde is cool," Froggy said.

"It was until I dropped the bottle, it broke on the floor, and everybody had to pussyfoot around the floor so they wouldn't get cut by the broken glass," I said.

"Oh." That's what Froggy said.

Okay, so I go on home and I'm feeling miserable. When I go to bed what fills up my dreams? Tommy throwing me the ball and me blowing the layup. Only in my dreams when the ball falls off the rim it breaks up on the floor and everybody on my team gets cut. When I get up in the morning I don't even want to go to school, but I go. You know, do the right thing and all that.

Froggy and I have biology together. All the way down the hall to class people were giving me dirty looks. We stopped to look at the posters for the junior dance and a girl gave me a bump in the back. I gave her a look and she gave me a look back.

"How you blow that layup?" she said. "You taking bribes or something?"

When she left I turned my attention back to the junior dance. "I'm thinking about asking Celia to the dance," I told Froggy.

"Celia *Evora*?" he asked.

"Yeah." Celia was from the Dominican Republic and the finest chick in the school.

"Man, you are never in all your days going to pull that girl," Froggy said. "You probably couldn't even pull her in a dream."

That got my jaw a little tight, but I didn't say anything. I just went on in and sat through the longest biology class I have ever had in my life. I thought the bell would never ring, but it finally did.

"Okay, class, let's wrap it up," Mr. Willis said. "This slide project is going to count as twenty-five percent of your final grade so I want the slides labeled with your name, class, and—"

My hands must have been sweaty. Maybe I caught a cramp in my fingers, I don't know. All I remember was a sick feeling to my stomach when the slide slipped out of my hand. I went to grab it and almost had it before it hit the ground. I looked up and Mr. Willis was looking down at me and shaking his head.

I had to explain to Mr. Willis how I didn't break the slide on purpose and he didn't believe a word of it. The man just looked at me and kept shaking his head. He picked up his marking book and I saw him write down a big red O next to my name.

"I'm giving up," I said to Froggy. "I'm going home, getting under my bed, and staying there until the year 3000. Maybe things won't be going so bad by then."

"You could be a streaker," Froggy said.

"A what?"

"A streaker," he said. "I read in this book that some people do things in streaks. You ever hear about a baseball player who gets a lot of hits in a row, then he stops and they don't get any more touchdowns?"

"You mean base hits?" I said.

"Whatever." Froggy shrugged. "Anyway, some people go through their whole lives like that. All of a sudden something really bad happens to you and then you do a bunch of bad things in a row. Or something good happens and you do a bunch of good things in a row. You lost the ball game, you broke the bottle in the locker room, then you just broke your slide in biology."

"I don't believe in luck or streaks or whatever else you're talking about," I said. We were taking a break in the cafeteria. I was having a soda and Froggy was drinking milk like he always did. "I don't believe in astrology, either."

Froggy kept on talking about this streak stuff but I wasn't into it. The next bell rang and we got up to leave. I dropped my soda can carefully into the garbage can. Then I grabbed Froggy's milk container and tossed it into the center of the can. I said center because I meant center. I don't know how it hit the edge of the can and bounced off into Maurice DuPre's lap.

Maurice DuPre is six feet high, six feet wide, and has more fingers and toes than he has points on his IQ. I watched as the last drops of milk fell onto Maurice's lap. Then I watched as he looked up at me with his little squinty, bloodshot eyes. Then I watched as he stood up with his fist in a ball. Then I ran out the cafeteria as fast as I could.

I spent all day sneaking around the halls and slipping into classrooms so Maurice wouldn't find me. I mean, I wasn't worried about fighting him, because I knew how it would come out. What I was worried about was if I would ever wake up when the fight was over.

When school was over I didn't even go to my locker to get my stuff. I just told Froggy to walk down the hall and if he saw Maurice to call out my name and point in some direction away from where I was sneaking out of a side door. Froggy didn't understand sports, but he understood me not wanting to get my butt kicked and so he went along with it. Last thing I heard in school was that Maurice was chasing Froggy around the gym.

I got to the block thinking about Froggy and Maurice and the streak. I stopped on the corner where I live and bought some potato wedgies and a soda from the burger joint. I got the wedgies first and started munching on them while the lady behind the counter poured my soda. Then I remembered I had taken my wallet out of my pocket and put it in my locker after lunch.

"These wedgies don't taste right!" I called out.

"They're going to taste a lot worse with a broken jaw," the manager called out. "So you just better pay up and eat them."

I knew by the time he got around the counter I could get away. All he got was one little whack at the back of my head that didn't even hurt.

Right home. Up the stairs, close the door and lock it, then cool out. Life was just wrong! The phone rang and I started not to answer it, but then the way things were working out I figured maybe it was somebody warning me that a killer was coming up the stairs to get me. I rushed to the phone, stopping just long enough to hit my ankle into a dumbbell. You ever hear that sound your anklebone makes when it hits steel? You ever see them little stars that go off in your head?

"Hello?"

"Jamie?" the voice on the phone asked.

"It depends," I said. "Who's this?"

"This is Mr. Bradley," came the answer. "I just wanted to let you know you failed your English test big-time. You're about a hair from failing the course. I just wanted to warn you."

"Oh, thank you, sir. You have made my day with your kindness," I said.

By the time I got to the refrigerator to get some ice for my ankle I was crying. No, I don't mean no sad look—I mean some right out boo-hooing with tears running down my face. My ankle was throbbing, my feelings were hurt, and I was ready to give it all up and resign from the human race.

I put the ice on my ankle, which was bruised and swollen and a little bloody. Then I sat down, put my leg up on the kitchen table, and called Froggy.

"Froggy, I give up, man," I said. "I'm on a death streak and I know I'm probably headed right on out the world."

"No, man, the streak is going to end," Froggy said.

"Yeah, when I'm dead."

"No," Froggy said. "Just like you missed the shot and lost the baseball game—"

"Basketball game," I said.

"Whatever. Anyway, something dramatic can happen and the whole thing will turn around. Then you'll have as much good luck as you had bad luck."

"What you mean by dramatic?" I asked.

"Hey, when it happens," Froggy said, "you'll know it."

Ellen is my sister. She's twelve and has a fast mouth. She also has braces that cost a whole bunch of money and I can't pop her when she's running her weak girl game.

"What happened to you?" she said when she came home. "I heard somebody was chasing you down the street?"

"Nothing," I said.

"Why don't you tell me who was chasing you so I can go tell them you're here?" she said.

"Why don't you shut up?" I answered.

"What happened to your leg?"

"Nothing."

She went to the refrigerator and took out the eggs. She took one egg out and handed it to me.

"Here," she said. "If nothing happened to your ankle you must have an egg under your skin it's sticking up so much. Here's another egg for your other leg."

Man, I just wanted to punch her right smack in her wire braces. She went waltzing out the kitchen and had the nerve to stick out her tongue at me. That's when I lost it. I tossed that egg toward the sink and started to get up but then the pain started throbbing in my leg and I sat back down real quick. I saw this movie once where this guy got shot in the leg and they had to cut it off. They gave him a drink of whiskey and a bullet to bite on. There was some soda in the fridge and I eased my leg down real slow and went for that. That's when I saw it.

Okay, wrap your brain around this. I got one hand on the refrigerator door when my mind hit the sink. I looked at the sink and there wasn't any egg in it. Then I looked at the carton of eggs on the counter and there were twelve eggs in the carton.

"Yo! Ellen! Come in here, quick!"

Ellen took her sweet time getting to the kitchen. Then she stood in the doorway with her hand on her skinny little hip. "What?"

"Did you hand me an egg a little while ago?" I asked.

"Jamie, are you using something you shouldn't be using?" she asked. "Like crack cocaine?"

"Did you hand me an egg or did you not hand me an egg?" I asked again.

"Yeah, you had an egg," she said. "Just don't get violent on me. You seeing any purple rabbits running around or things like that?"

"Check this out," I said. I knew I was excited. "I threw the egg over here and it landed in the egg carton!"

"Isn't that sweet."

"No, you don't understand," I said. "First the telephone was ringing and then I hit my leg on the dumbbell and then I failed English, see?"

"You really enjoy yourself when you're alone, huh?"

Okay, so the girl was seriously stupid. But I knew who would understand and I called Froggy back and told him what happened.

"How many bad things happened to you?" Froggy asked.

"A thousand," I said.

"No, exactly how many bad things happened to you?" he said. "We need the exact number."

I started counting. I missed the shot in the basketball game, that was the first thing. Then I broke the bottle in the locker room. The third thing was when I broke the slide in biology.

"Then you dumped milk on Maurice DuPre," Froggy said. "He's still looking for you."

"Right, then I left my wallet in school and couldn't pay for my potato wedgies. Then when I got home I banged up my ankle and found out that I flunked my English test."

"Seven things," Froggy said. "Now you have seven pieces of good luck coming your way."

"Wait a minute," I said. "I just found out that I

failed the English test. I didn't actually fail it at that time."

"When did you take it?"

"Just before the . . . just before the basketball game," I said.

"Okay, now you just had one piece of good luck because you threw the egg toward the sink and it landed in the carton," Froggy said. "You have six to go."

"I'm going for the top right away," I said. "I'm asking Celia to the dance."

"Hey, go for it."

I figured I'd see Celia in school and pop the question. The whole scene was in my mind. Celia would be coming down the hall with one of those short little skirts she wears, looking tan and sweet and with those fine legs of hers strutting like she owned the world. Then I would call her name and say, "Hey, we *are* going to the dance together?" and she would just kind of go into a half swoon and maybe giggle a little and it would be all set.

When I got to school I was feeling good. Math was the first class and we had one of Galicki's famous pop quizzes. I was sitting in the back of the room where I always sit and dreaming about laying some serious lip on Celia when I heard Mr. Galicki calling my name.

"Yeah, wazzup?"

"I said"—Mr. Galicki raised his voice—"that I'm really surprised that you did so well on the pop quiz. You really understand parallelograms."

Hey, what can I tell you? I met Froggy, who was coming from band practice, and told him the good news.

"That's two things," he said. "You got five left."

"That wasn't luck," I said.

"Math?" Froggy said. "You're good in math?"

It was luck. I had to be careful. I needed to get a yes from Celia before I used up my streak. I stopped right there in the hallway and told myself to calm down.

"Calm down and think hard, my Nubian selfhood."

I needed a soda. I went to the cafeteria, looked around to see if Maurice was there, saw he wasn't, and went and dropped a quarter in the machine.

"Yo, it ain't working!" Tommy from the ball team called to me. "It takes your money, but you don't get a soda!"

I had only put in a quarter, but the machine was whirring and humming. Then a bottle of soda came down.

The guys came over and started pounding on the machine, but nothing happened for them. That was my third lucky thing on my streak. I had four to go.

Okay, I had to go for the big time. Celia was from Santiago, DR. Just looking at her made me want to move to the Dominican Republic. I decided to go the whole nine with her, flowers and everything. The plan was this. I buy some roses, take them over to her house, which is up on 153rd and Broadway, give her the roses, and ask her to the dance. There's a guy on 135th who sells roses, so I bought six. A dozen sounds good but six is cool.

Then I get a little nervous. Celia can make you nervous because she is so fine. Anyway, girls make me a little uptight. But I'm working on the streak so everything is everything. I buy the roses, and I come home. Ellen is checking me out and I tell her to mind her business. Then I call Celia's number, which I had gotten from Ramona Rodriguez, who is also fine, but she goes with Paco, and nobody messes with Paco.

"Hello? Mrs. Evora? This is Jamie Farrell. Is Celia there?"

"Who?"

"Jamie Farrell," I repeated. "I go to school with Celia."

"Oh, she had to go to the doctor," Mrs. Evora said. "She has an allergy to certain flowers and she has to take treatments."

"Roses?" I asked.

"She told you?"

"Something like that," I said. "Will you tell her Jamie called?"

"Yes, Gamie called to find out about her allergy," she said.

Right. Gamie called to find out about her allergy. I gave the flowers to my mother. That was four good things that happened. But the flowers cost me a lot and if I was going to take Celia to the dance I'd at least need money to stop for something to eat afterward and a taxi to get her home.

My streak was running low and I was getting nervous. I still hadn't actually asked Celia to go to the dance with me.

"So just do it," Froggy said. "Walk up to her and say, 'Hey, mama, let's you and me start working on the *lambada* so we look good for the natives at the dance.'"

"What's the lam—what did you call it?"

"Call the chick quick," Froggy said.

So I'm lying in bed listening to the news, which sounds like the same thing they've been telling us for the last year, so I don't see why it's news, when there's a knock on my door. I figure it's Ellen coming to borrow something, so I don't say anything. Then the door opens and it's my dad and he flicks the light on.

"Can I talk to you?" he asks.

"Yeah, sure," I say. I'm wondering if he ever dated a Dominican fox.

"Son, I want to talk to you about drugs."

He never dated a Dominican fox, I think. He must have got lucky with Mom.

Then my dad breaks into this whole rap about how bad drugs are and it's like we're making a television commercial or something. All the time I'm wondering how I'm going to get the money to take Celia home in a taxi and if I could make a move on her in the back of the taxi.

"I know that so many young men living in the inner city feel deprived of the better things in life," my dad was saying. "Son, I'm going to give you this hundred dollars so you won't feel that way. And I'm asking you, in return, to come and talk to me about anything that bothers you. You seem so depressed lately. I won't push it, though. I'll wait for you."

That was the fifth thing in the streak. My dad giving me a hundred dollars just when I needed money. I was in desperate trouble.

I had to concentrate on Celia. Celia, with the dark eyes and the nice boobs. I was in love with her and I had this one shot, this one streak to get her to go to the dance with me. Concentrate. Concentrate on Celia.

I called Froggy.

"You're in trouble," he said. "Your streak is jumbling up on you."

"What's that mean?" I asked.

"It's out of control," he said. "You're probably just naturally lucky, so your luck is coming too fast."

Nothing. That was what I was going to do until I got Celia on the phone and asked her to the dance. Nothing. Lie on the bed. Nothing. I wasn't even going to think of anything. I got a sheet of paper and wrote down all the good things that had happened to me. Then I realized that I was doing something that could result in good luck. I was lying on the bed and lifted my head until I could see my wastebasket. I tossed a high, arcing shot toward the basket.

Panic! I dove for the paper to knock it away! I didn't want this to be my next lucky thing. I hit it up in the air just before it went into the basket. Then the door opened and knocked the paper against the wall just over my Malcolm X poster, against the side of my dresser, and into the wastebasket.

"What is wrong with you?" Ellen stood in the doorway. "Are you, like, freaking out or something?"

I called Froggy.

"Did you want the paper to go into the basket?" he asked.

"Not when I realized it was going to be my sixth lucky thing," I said.

"But when you threw it, you did, right?" Froggy asked.

I hung up and made a note to myself that I did not like Froggy.

Okay, get the picture. I'm in school and I'm running out of luck. I've got one shot left on my streak.

And my school, Ralph Bunche, is playing against Carver. We're not supposed to beat Carver. But I'm worried and I tell the coach that my ankle is hurt and I can't play. He looks at the ankle and it's still swollen and he says okay. I'm on the bench.

Carver is supposed to kill us. They've got guys on that team that are fifteen, maybe sixteen feet tall. But somehow our team stays with them and I'm praying that us winning with me not even playing is not my last lucky event. I figured no way that could happen. But then our guys, really going all out, are playing Carver so tough that the game is just about even. But some of our key guys are fouling out. It gets down to the end of the game and the coach turns to me.

"Either you play or we only have four players and we lose for certain," he said.

Just don't shoot, I think.

I remembered how this whole thing began. Fifteen seconds to go against Powell Academy and me running toward the basket and then missing the shot. I want us to win this game but I want to go to a dance with Celia even more.

I looked up at the clock. Nine seconds. I looked up at the scoreboard. Carver 47, Ralph Bunche 46. Don't shoot, I said to myself. Just don't shoot. Think of Celia. Dark eyes. Short skirt. Beautiful teeth. Nice boobs.

"We've got one chance in a million," the coach said. "We'll go with the thirty-four play to Tommy. Jerry inbounds the ball to Tommy and everybody else blocks out their man the best they can."

"Good choice, Coach," I said.

Jerry inbounded the ball or, at least, he tried to inbound the ball. A Carver guy knocked it away and it came to me. I picked it up and saw Tommy sliding inside. Two huge dudes from Carver came after me. I needed to get the ball to Tommy and threw it over their outstretched fingers. The ball went up, and up, and up. The buzzer went off as the ball went down and the referee pointed to it. The last shot of the game. Only it wasn't a shot. It really wasn't a shot. It really, really, *really* wasn't a shot even as it came down through the net.

They carried me off the court and, to tell the truth, it felt pretty good. But I had blown my one chance with Celia.

The next day in school everybody was talking about how I had won the game and everything and how cool I was with it. What I was waiting for was my new streak to begin. So I'm walking down the hall and who's coming down the hall with two of her girlfriends but none other than Celia Evora, Her Loveliness.

"Nice game," she says to me. Her teeth are like sparkling and her eyes are like flashing and my heart is beating like crazy but I know the score.

"It was luck," I said.

"My mom told me you called," she said.

"Just wanted to see how you were doing," I said. "Your mom said you had an allergy."

"Yes, and I wanted to talk to you about something," she said.

"What?"

"You going with anybody to the junior dance?" she asked.

"I hadn't thought about it," I said.

"You want to go with me?" she asked.

"Sure," I said.

"I *knew* you would say yes," she said. "I just knew it."

"You did?"

"Sure. This is my lucky week. Figure it out. The hospital finally figured out what I'm allergic to, and I passed every test I took in school. Then, just after my mom said I couldn't go to the dance because she didn't trust any of the boys, you called to find out about my allergy and she said you had to be the nicest boy in the school and if I went with you I could go. Am I lucky or what?"

"It sounds like you're on a streak," I said.

"I hope it never ends!" she said. "Pick me up early for the dance."

Celia turned her head, flashed those dark eyes at me, and danced her way down the hall.

Froggy saw me standing in the hallway leaning against the wall.

"What happened?" he asked. "You okay?"

"I just figured out that the whole world is on a streak," I said.

"What does that mean?" Froggy asked.

Froggy went on about what the word *streak* meant. I really didn't care anymore. It was all good.

Monkeyman

The Tigros hit the 'hood gradually, like the turning of a season. First we saw some tags scrawled on the wall near the Pioneer Supermarket. Then we heard that a kid on 141st Street got stabbed and they arrested a member of a gang called Tigros.

"What's that supposed to mean?" Fee asked. "What's a Tigro, anyway?"

I didn't know. I didn't even want to talk about gangs. Some people said—okay, it wasn't some people, it was my uncle who runs the barbershop—Uncle Duke said that I had a bad attitude about Harlem.

"You're so anxious to leave you're not even giving your homeland a chance," he said.

"Africa is my homeland," I said.

"That's the easy answer, isn't it?" he said. He was

sweeping the floor of the shop. "Like running away from the neighborhood."

He was right, really. Fee, who is my main man, said that I had black skin and white dreams, that all I wanted to do was to get away someplace and be with white people.

I liked a lot of things about Harlem, especially the block, which was how we talked about 145th Street. There were good people on the block, but what I wanted was to be more than what I saw on the block. Uncle Duke said I could be more, but if I put Harlem out of my heart I could end up being a lot less, too.

Yeah, well, I was ready to take my chances. What I wanted to do was to be a doctor and have a nice crib, and a Benz, the whole nine. Then the thing happened with Monkeyman.

Monkeyman was always quiet. He was down with the books and everything, but he kept to himself a lot and didn't get into anybody else's business. We used to call him Monkeyman because sometimes he would go to the park, climb up into a tree, and sit up there and read all day. We weren't dissing him, we just gave him the tag and he seemed to like it, so it stuck.

Anyway, the Tigros turned out to be a new gang that were trying to build a rep in the 'hood. They were biting all the stuff they read in the papers about wearing colors and flashing signs and whatnot. It wasn't a real big thing until they started terrorizing stores and then they beat up a lot of people and stabbed that one kid. After that you saw their tag all over the place, like stabbing a kid was something to be proud of.

What usually happens when a new gang makes the scene is they jump bad as a posse for a while until they step too far and their leaders get busted. Then, when they realize that their reps and tattoos and colors don't keep them out of jail, they chill and their colors fade. But that hadn't happened yet with the Tigros. They were still wilding and messing with people and putting out squad tracts. A squad tract is when somebody messes with a posse and they let everybody know they're going to kick his butt. When the word comes down that a gang is after you it's scary, and one of the reasons I wanted to leave the area.

Okay, so here's what happened with Monkeyman and the Tigros. It started when one of the Lady Tigros got into a beef with Peaches. The Lady Tigros were just as bad as the dudes and one of them slapped Peaches in the face. Peaches and the girl got into it pretty good and Peaches won the fight. Then, on the way home, two of the Lady Tigros went after Peaches and one of them had a razor blade. Monkeyman was coming from school and had stopped off to buy a soda on the ave. He saw the girl trying to cut Peaches and he ran out and knocked the blade from the girl's hand. Bingo, the fight's over because neither of those two girls wanted to mess with Peaches without a blade and they weren't on their turf anyway. But one of the Lady Tigros went to the same school as Monkeyman. She went back and told the Tigros and before you knew it everybody on the block was talking about how Monkeyman was in big trouble.

There were signs painted on the walls—MONKEYMAN

MUST DIE! and MONKEYMAN GOT TO FALL! It was all signed by the Tigros.

Uncle Duke saw Monkeyman in the barbershop and told him to lay low for a while. Fee told him the same thing but everybody figured that Monkeyman was going to get beat up and maybe even worse.

"You know any karate or anything?" I asked Monkeyman when I ran into him on the corner.

"I read a book on it once," he said.

"That's not good enough," I said.

He shrugged and gave me this little grin. Okay, let me back up a little. Monkeyman is six feet tall, maybe even six feet one, and thin. He plays a little ball but he's really not kicking hoops and he's kind of mild-looking. He's not a lame or anything like that but he's more down with his mind than his hands. So we worried about him.

"We need to get together and help Monkeyman," Peaches said.

"That's hip," Fee said. "It's hip to help a brother in trouble and everything, but what you're talking about is getting a posse together to go down with the Tigros and that's heavier than it is hip."

"We can tell the police," Peaches said.

"A guy I know went to the police when he got into trouble with a numbers runner," I said. "The numbers runner said he was going to cut him a new place to pee from. He went to the police and the police told him they couldn't do anything until something happened."

"They're into cutting people," Peaches said. "That's serious."

"Yo, Peaches, I didn't know you were sweating Monkeyman," Fee said.

"Lighten up, lame," Peaches came back with her quick mouth. "Monkeyman had the heart to help me when I needed some help. If you don't have the heart to help him that's cool, but don't try to finesse it off like it's no big thing."

"He needs a gun," Fee said. "That's the only thing they respect."

Just blow the word and I was ready to split. From a scrap in the street the jam was jumping to nines. On the way home I tried thinking about what Monkeyman could do. If the Tigros came on him and just beat him up it would be cool. I mean, that was sick but it was better than being cut or shot. And the thing was that a lot of kids were talking about being down with gangs and trying to make themselves large by going to wack city and offing somebody. That was the danger big-time. To me it was like some moron jumping off a big building and styling for the camera on the way down. They would be throwing away their life, and taking somebody else's life for some moment they imagined would happen. This craziness filled my nightmares. And it might have been sad but the truth was that I was glad it was Monkeyman on the line, and not me.

Two weeks passed from the time that Monkeyman had stopped the girl from cutting Peaches and it looked as if things might blow over without anyone getting hurt. Then a guy called Clean entered the picture.

Ralph J. Bunche is the best school in the 'hood but

every so often we get in a guy who doesn't fit. That's what Clean was. He wasn't a big dude, more small and wiry. He wore his pants low in hip-hop style with about four inches of his shorts showing. You're not allowed to style down in the school but he kept at it and the hallway teachers got on his case. He told everyone he was from L.A. and used to run with the Crips, but Fee peeped his school record and the dude was really from some place in California called Lompoc.

Clean hooked up with some folks who told him about the Tigros posse. Check this out, to get into the Tigros you either had to slash a saint in public, meaning cut somebody who wasn't involved in nothing, just walking down the street, or make something that was foul righteous. According to the Tigros posse, since Monkeyman had messed with them and that was foul, getting even with him was making it righteous.

It got around in the cafeteria that Clean was going to do up Monkeyman. Peaches was still trying to settle things peacefully.

"Let's just go up to the dude and see if we can talk a hole in his ego or whatever else it takes," she said. "Because I got to be watching Monkeyman's back the same way he turned out for me."

A few other kids said they were willing to try to talk to Clean. But the truth is that some dudes you can talk to and some you can't. In the first place Clean was not into brain surgery. I mean, his favorite sentence was "Huh?" Clean was in a class called ZIP. ZIP was supposed to stand for Zoned for Individual Progress, but all the kids called it the Underground Railroad because it was the last stop you made before you dropped out of high school.

Okay, besides Clean not being a brainiac he was also like nine shades of serious wack. He was the kind of kid who made you wonder what his mama had been smoking when he was in the womb. But, hey, give it a shot, right?

We found him on the street, and Peaches took the first shot at Clean. "So," she said, "there's no use in us, as young black brothers and sisters, getting into the same violence thing that's killing us off and messing up our dreams. If we can't respect each other, how are we going to expect people to respect us?"

"He messed with the Tigros so he got to be messed up!" Clean answered.

"Why?" came out of me before I could stop it.

"Because that's the way it goes!" Clean said. "He got to be messed up!"

I could see that Clean was getting off with everybody standing around trying to cop a plea for Monkeyman. We split the session and I was still hoping that things would blow over. For Monkeyman's sake and for Peaches' sake, too.

The next day Clean got busted bringing a knife to school. If you bring any kind of weapon to Bunche it means an automatic suspension and then you have to go through the bring-in-your-parents bit to get back in. When Mr. Aumack, the principal, called the police,

Clean got mad and walked out of the school. But before he left he sent word that he'd be waiting for Monkeyman when we got out at three-fifteen.

Three-fifteen came. When we looked out of the windows, we saw about a dozen Tigros outside. They were all wearing their black do-rags and some of them had jackets with their tag on them.

Mr. Aumack called the police again and in a few minutes the whole block was filled with squad cars. Their lights were flashing and police were snatching everybody wearing Tigros gear. One of the Tigros spotted Monkeyman and got up in his face. He said, "When we catch you we'll cap you."

"How about tomorrow night, eleven o'clock in Jackie Robinson Memorial Park?" Monkeyman said.

"Bet!" the Tigros dude said. "Tomorrow night in the park. Be there, sucker, and wear something that's going to look good at the autopsy."

"And bring your whole posse," Monkeyman said.

Whoa. Monkeyman had called out Tigros big-time. I grabbed his arm and we started walking away.

If you're going to get into somebody's face you got to know they got a mind somewhere behind their eyebrows. Then maybe they'll do some heavy thinking and settle for a chill pill.

"What you doing, Monkeyman?" I asked.

"What's got to be done," Monkeyman said. "Just what's got to be done."

The word bounced around: Be in the park to catch the go-down at eleven. Some kids said they didn't want any part of it.

"Let's kidnap Monkeyman," Fee said. "He don't show and nothing can happen."

It was all gums and teeth because nobody really knew what to do. I was all for dropping a dime to 911 but everyone else said no.

"I'm going to be at the park," Peaches said.

Fee said he would be, too. So did Tommy Collins, Debbie, LaToya, Jamie, and me. I didn't want to show, but Peaches made it clear that anybody that didn't would be punking out.

We hadn't seen Monkeyman all day and rumors were that he had left town.

"Maybe he'll show at the last minute with an Uzi and start blowing away all the Tigros," LaToya said.

Nobody said anything when we headed up the hill to the park. I wondered if everybody else could hear their heart beating. I was wearing my sneakers, ready to run if I had to.

When we got to the park there were maybe twenty-five guys in their Tigros gear and ten girls.

My knees got real loose and I was having trouble swallowing.

"Where Monkeyman?" Clean asked. He was wearing a heavy jacket and had his hands in his pockets. "Where Monkeyman?"

"We thought he was here," Fee said. I noticed Fee's voice was kind of high.

We waited for another ten or fifteen minutes with all

the Tigros posse calling us suckers and stuff like that. I was hoping they didn't turn on us.

"Yo, here he come now!" A girl pointed toward the uptown side of the park. "Who he got with him?"

I turned and I saw Monkeyman coming down the street. He had a man and a woman with him. The man looked old. Monkeyman brought them right over to where we were and I recognized his grandfather. I didn't know the woman.

"Hey, this is my grandfather," Monkeyman said. "His name is Mr. Nesbitt. And this is my godmother, Sister Smith."

"What you bring them for?" Clean said, edging closer to Monkeyman.

"They came to see you mess me up!" Monkeyman said.

He took off his jacket as if he meant to fight Clean. For a moment I thought maybe it would be a fair fight. But then Monkeyman took off his shirt and just stood there in his bare skin and held his hands out and his head to one side.

Clean didn't know what was happening. He looked around.

"Kick his butt!" one of the Tigros called out. "Waste him!"

Clean took his hands out of his pockets and started circling Monkeyman, but Monkeyman didn't move. Clean hit him in the back of his head and he didn't say nothing.

"Please don't do that, boy," Monkeyman's grandfather said. "He made us promise not to help him, but please don't do that."

"We'll kick your butt, too," a girl said.

Everybody turned and looked at her and she held out her chin like she didn't even care. But she didn't say anything else.

Monkeyman's godmother was praying.

It was dark but there was a moon out and the park lights were on. More people came into the park to see what was going on. What they saw was Monkeyman standing with his arms outstretched and Clean hitting him. He hit him in the face a couple of times and an old man asked, "What's going on?"

"That's the Tigros gang," Fee said. "They're beating up Monkeyman because he stopped one of their girls from slashing somebody in the face."

"I ought to kill you!" Clean shouted.

"They just waiting for the police to come," another Tigros guy said.

It grew quiet. There had to be fifty people watching now, watching Clean standing in front of Monkeyman, not knowing what to do, watching the rest of the gang not knowing where to take it, watching Monkeyman with his arms still out from his sides, his nose bleeding, his body quivering from the pain and from the growing cold. The high streetlamps outside the park cast a pale glare on Monkeyman's dark skin. The shadow on the ground, of Monkeyman's body being offered up for a beating, was long and thin and disappeared into the shifting knot of people watching.

"That's what's wrong with the neighborhood now," a man said. "We got it hard enough without this kind of thing."

"He ain't nothing but a punk." A short, squat guy stepped out from the Tigros group. "If he don't fight he a punk!"

"I ain't even going to waste my time on him," Clean said. "If I was back in the Crips I wouldn't even waste my time on no punk."

The Tigros were outnumbered now, and began drifting off. When they got down to the last five or so someone yelled that the cops were coming and they all ran.

Monkeyman put on his shirt. His grandfather put his arm around him and they started out of the park. The wind picked up a little and I began to shiver. Around me others were slowly starting to move and I pulled my jacket shut and started home.

I saw Monkeyman two days later.

"You were wrong," I said. "You took a chance and you could have been killed."

"I was hurt," Monkeyman said. "I was hurt but they were wrong, not me."

"What if they had killed you?" I said.

He just looked at me. "I know," he said. "I know."

He said it with a sadness that just got all into me. He had been looking down but now Monkeyman looked up, right into my eyes, as if he expected me to say something that was right for the moment. I couldn't think of anything.

"Yo, Monkeyman, what did you think was going to happen that night?" I asked.

"I just thought that some people were going to show wrong, and some others were going to show right," he said. "No matter what happened to me, everybody was going to know the difference."

I couldn't see it. I wouldn't have let them beat on me like that. What I would have done I don't know.

It didn't end there. Three weeks later another guy in the Tigros stabbed Monkeyman in the back. Monkeyman was in the hospital for three weeks, hanging on between life and death, but finally he made it.

The guy who stabbed Monkeyman had been arrested before for possession of drugs and was on parole. They gave him ten to fifteen years for attempted murder. So Monkeyman got hurt and the guy that hurt him would be in jail until he wasn't a kid anymore.

It was all so scary. All so sad.

I went to visit Monkeyman in the hospital. We talked about what was going on in school, and what was going on around the 'hood.

"Man, I can't wait to go to college," I said. "I need to put some serious distance between me and 145th Street. How about you?"

"I got accepted at an art school in Pittsburgh," he said. "When I get finished I'll probably come back and open a studio or something. How about you?"

"I don't know," I said. "When I get to be a doctor maybe I'll come back and take care of guys like you."

Monkeyman grinned.

When I left I looked back over everything that had happened. What he did in the park wasn't smart. As a matter of fact it was dumb. Maybe. But as Peaches always said, when you have a friend like Monkeyman, somebody has to watch his back. I thought about what had happened in the park for months afterward. That night in the park Monkeyman had seemed so small, but now, in my mind and in my heart, he has grown. Yeah, Monkeyman.

Kitty and Mack:
A Love Story

Eddie McCormick was all-world and everybody knew it. While most of the guys on the block played basketball, Mack, which was what everybody called him, played baseball. He played left field for the Ralph Bunche Academy and when they played there would be more scouts in the stands than fans. He was big, a hundred and eighty pounds and six feet one. During the winter he ran track and the track coach thought he could make the Olympics if he stuck with sprinting. The coach kept him on the team even when he wasn't running, just in case he might show up at a meet. But baseball was Mack's joint and that was where he figured to be headed. He was eighteen and one newspaper article about him said that he could be in the major leagues by the time he was nineteen. That's how good he was. Naturally the baseball coach loved him. That was the thing about Mack, the people who liked him usually liked him because he was a star. Mack had an attitude problem. He thought he could just show up and everybody was supposed to fall down and go crazy or something.

He was pretty smart, too, but he made this big show of not caring about grades. He slid into his senior year with a C-minus average.

"If they gave him what he really deserved," Dottie Lynch said, "he would be getting all P's. That's *P* as in *pitiful*."

Well, Dottie had a big mouth but that's what people thought about Mack. Some of the kids thought that Dottie was sweating Mack and was just mad because he didn't give her a play. On the other hand everybody thought he was stuck on himself. But during the first week of his senior year everything changed. That's when he met Kitty.

Kitty was the granddaughter of Duke Wilson, who owned the barbershop on 145th across from Grace Tabernacle Church. Now, anybody who knew Mr. Wilson would expect his granddaughter to be smart, but Kitty was outrageous. Just the way that Mack dealt with baseball and had all the scouts looking at him, Kitty could deal with the books. What's more, everybody liked Kitty because she had one of those bubbling kind of personalities that soon as you met her you knew she was your flavor. Plus, the girl was fine. Not just kind of fine, not just take another look fine, but, like, take the batteries out of the smoke alarms when she came by fine. Yeah, that's right. So she's smart, she's fine, she's only sixteen and a senior.

Okay, the first week of school Mrs. Henry, our English teacher, said we had to write poems in the style of some famous poet. And you had to write the poem to a particular person.

"It can be someone you admire," Mrs. Henry said. "Someone you're in love with, or even someone to whom you just want to send a message."

The boys all treated the assignment like it was a big goof and most of the girls weren't too excited about it, either. On the day the poems were read in class it was mostly funny stuff or poems about how they loved their mothers. Three people wrote poems about Martin Luther King, Jr. Half the class just listened to the poems and hoped they wouldn't be called on to read theirs out loud. But when it was time for Kitty to read her poem, she said, "I'm going to read my poem to Mack."

Everybody paid attention.

Mack leaned back in his seat and got this look on his face like he was too cool to breathe. Okay, Kitty went and stood right in front of Mack and started reciting her poem real slow. She was just glancing at the paper it was written on but most of the time she was looking dead into Mack's eyes.

> *"How do I love thee, you sweet black thing*
> *Why do I love thee, is this some fling*
> *That my wildly beating heart has chanced*
> *Upon or has my light and joyous soul danced*
> *With yours in some other life or taken wing*
> *And flown with yours, you sweet black thing."*

The class was quiet and Mrs. Henry put her book down and sat behind her desk. Kitty went on with her poem.

"How do I love thee, my sweet black prince
For surely I have loved thee ever since
My eyes first met your fierce but tender gaze
And your gentle touch did expand my days
As poets' songs fulfill the singing verse
And sweet love fulfills the universe.

"I haven't finished it yet," Kitty said. "It's going to be a sonnet."

She hadn't finished the sonnet but she had finished Mack. From that minute on he was stupid in love. What she did was to flat-out change the brother. She had reached inside him and took out his attitude. Peewee put it best.

"What Mack was doing was dealing wrong but dealing so strong you couldn't do nothing about it," he said. "But how strong can you be when some girl can make you roll over and play dead any time she wants to? She can make that dude fetch like a cocker spaniel if she wanted."

That was true, because Mack would be in the cafeteria or walking down the hallway and all of a sudden this silly grin would come over his face and either Kitty would be someplace near or he would be thinking about her. Mack was so much in love that it made people feel good just to be around him. He was talking about going right to the major leagues and playing pro ball while Kitty went to school.

They went out steady for a while and after a few weeks Kitty naturally wanted to know how Mack felt about her. She hinted around for a while, then she came right out and asked him.

"You're okay," he said.

"Don't give me no okay," Kitty said. "I want to know if you love me."

"Something like that," Mack said.

That's what he said to Kitty, but to everybody else he was planning his whole life.

"It'll take her six or seven years to get her law degree," he said. "Then I'll play ball for another eight or nine years and then we'll open a little business."

Kitty lived with her parents above her grandfather's shop. That's where Mack was coming from the day before Christmas. Kitty had been up at Brown University in Rhode Island on a visit to see if she wanted to go to that school and Mack had met her at the train station. It was a cold night and a light snow was falling. Down on the corner some guys were selling Christmas trees and had started a fire in a garbage can to keep warm.

All of a sudden two guys come running down the street. They were hoofing heavy and looking back over their shoulders. When they ran across Powell Avenue they almost got hit by a gypsy cab. The cab swerved just in time and one brother was slipping on the snow and almost fell in the path of a delivery truck. He was so close to being hit that he steadied himself on the fender of the truck. The car that came across the intersection was an old Mustang painted black. The two guys were running on the uptown side of the street but the Mustang came over, facing the wrong way in traffic, and a dude leaned out the back window.

"Drive-by!" a kid screamed.

People were hitting the ground, or running, or ducking behind cars. Most of them didn't know where the shooting was coming from. A window broke, sending glass across the sidewalk. People screamed. Tires squealed. The two guys they were shooting at turned the corner and ran up the avenue. The car sped away toward the bridge that leads to the Bronx. In a minute it was out of sight.

"That's a shame!" an old West Indian woman was saying.

"Those gang people don't care two cents for your life!" the woman with her said.

"The day before Christmas, too," the first woman went on, shaking her head. "They don't have a thing to do but to—is that somebody laying on the ground over there?"

It was Mack. A man called the police and in minutes the street was full of police cars and emergency vehicles.

"He's moving," a long-headed boy with a scarf around his face said. "He's okay."

They took Mack downtown to Harlem Hospital. Pookie, who came along after the shooting and saw that it was Mack, went and told his folks.

It was Christmas day when the news got back to the block. Mack was going to live, but two bullets had torn into his right ankle and just about taken his foot off. Doctors had worked on his foot for seven hours, but finally they gave up. It had to be amputated.

When he came out of the hospital Mack was different. It wasn't like he just acted a little strange; he was a different person. At first when some of the guys went around to see him they said he didn't talk much, but then after a while he wouldn't even come out of his room. Then Peewee found out that he hadn't seen Kitty.

"She didn't even go to the hospital?" Eddie, who was in Mack's math class, asked.

"She went to the hospital," Peewee said. "But since he's been home he hasn't seen her. He told his mother not to let her in and he won't answer the phone."

"You can't turn your back on people like that," Eddie answered.

But the truth was that Mack could turn his back on people, because he really had turned his back on himself. Kitty called him every day at the same time so he would know it was her, but he wouldn't answer.

Mack's father worked in a restaurant just down from Sylvia's. It wasn't as high-class a restaurant as Sylvia's but it was nice. He went to work at one in the afternoon and Mack would keep his door closed, not even come out of his room, until after his father had left.

The next thing that Kitty did was to organize a little get-together with Peewee and some of the guys on the baseball team. Peewee told me about it and for the first time he didn't make a lot of jokes about it.

"He was sitting on his bed and he had his leg out from under the cover," Peewee said. "You know, we just sat there and tried not to look at his leg. Mack kept laughing at his leg and pointing to it. Man, it was terrible. Dottie was there and she held Kitty's hand."

"She was tore up," Dottie said. "You loving somebody like she loves that fool and you hate to see them looking so pitiful."

"Nobody else could get it up to say anything," Peewee continued. "People started drifting out one by one. I know those guys aren't going back there. That scene was too rough."

No one saw Mack for a long time after that. There were reports that he had lost a lot of weight, and that maybe he was losing his mind. The worst time was when Mack's father called the cops because he wouldn't come down from the roof. It was nearly three o'clock in the morning in late January. A cold rain slanted down onto the tar paper and onto the lone figure sitting on the ledge overlooking the empty street below. A policeman tried to talk him away from the edge but Mack didn't respond.

"Why, son, why?" his father pleaded with him. "You're young and still got your whole thing going on in front of you. I know it's not like it was but you're still young."

"Who?" Mack spoke without moving.

At first his father just looked at him, not knowing what his son was getting at. "What you mean who?" his father asked.

"Who are you talking to?"

"I'm talking to you, son," his father said.

"I'm not your son," Mack said. "Your son was a ballplayer, wasn't he? He didn't have no missing parts, did he?"

"You're hurt, but . . ." His father's voice trailed off. The pain sat between them even as the rain beat down harder, releasing the stench of dog urine from the cracks in the roof.

The policemen told Mack's parents that they could either try to pull him down or leave and see if he could be talked down. Mack's father said he'd stay with him and try to talk him down.

It was almost dawn when Mack, shaking with cold and the rage of frustration, finally got up and walked to the stairwell. Kitty was sitting on the stairs, a blanket around her shoulders. Mack stopped for a moment and Kitty took his hand. It was trembling as she put it against her face. Without speaking he pulled it away, and, leaning against the sagging banister, went down the stairs.

"He's not going to last," Kitty's grandfather said later. "The boy has lost his will to live."

The first week of February was as cold as it could be in the city without completely freezing over. There was a heavy snow on the weekend that blanketed the block in a crisp white silence. Neon signs that seemed good-humored and inviting during warm weather turned cool and distant.

Old men and women walked carefully along the slick

sidewalks. Younger people leaned into the wind that swirled along the edges of the buildings. In the mornings there were flurries of young mothers taking their bundled children to old mothers who would care for them during the day.

Mentions of Mack had grown fewer and fewer until the morning Kitty showed up at nine o'clock at Duke's Barbershop.

"Why aren't you in school?" Duke asked.

"I decided to stay home from now on and take care of Mack," Kitty said.

"That's kind of rough, isn't it?" Duke said. "You know how important school is."

"Not that rough," Kitty said. "I can handle it. When things get right I'll go back."

"Kitty . . ." Duke took his granddaughter by the hand and led her to one of the barber chairs. He sat her down and took both her hands in his. "Honey, life goes on even when some of us decide to stop and rest along the way. Mack's young, but he's a man, and he's made a decision about his life. If he doesn't want help you can't give it to him."

"Then why am I going to school?" Kitty asked. "What can I study that's so important that I'm supposed to leave people who need me?"

"Girl, you're smart enough to know everything your grandfather is going to say," Duke said. "I'll call his dad and see if he'll let you come up and see him. From what I heard he's not eating or anything. But if he won't see you I think you should go on back to school."

"I'm not going to see him," Kitty answered. "I'm

just going to let him know I'm here to take care of him."

"You what?" Duke sat down in the other chair. The door opened and Duke told the customer that he was closed.

Of course everybody on the block soon knew that Kitty was staying home from school. After all the talk about how smart she was there was a lot of surprise and some people were saying that maybe she wasn't as smart as people thought.

"You don't give up your education for some guy who won't even talk to you," Peaches said. "And she didn't go up to his house or nothing. She just put a letter in the window of Duke's place saying that she was going to be there and waiting for Mack to come to see her."

The letter was printed on big cardboard. It wasn't anything fancy, either.

Mack,

I'm home from school. I'm here at Duke's Barbershop every day and I'm waiting for you to tell you how much I love you.

Kitty

Now, that letter seemed strange at first because it was written to Mack but it was never sent to him. It was also strange to put the letter in the window where everybody could see it. That was getting the whole block in your business. People were divided in their thinking. Some people felt that maybe there was something wrong with Kitty, too. Earl said that sometimes love drove people crazy, but Sadie, Peaches' mama, said the girl was just too young to know better. Of course she didn't say it in front of Kitty's mama, who was really upset about the whole thing. Kitty's father even demanded that she go back to school at once, but Kitty said she wasn't going to go even if it meant she had to move out and be homeless. We all knew that Duke wouldn't let her be on the street.

Everybody was busting to tell Mack about Kitty sitting in Duke's place every day waiting for him to come down. The first thing that happened was that his mother came by and told Kitty that she was wasting her time.

"You're such a sweet girl," Mrs. McCormick said. "But he's so despondent he doesn't want to do anything."

"That's his problem," Kitty said. "My problem is staying here waiting for him."

A guidance counselor came by and gave Kitty her sternest voice and shook several of her fingers at her. But Kitty wouldn't budge and, as far as the school was concerned, it was a matter of were they going to suspend Kitty or let her finish and go on to college.

Time went by and it was the third of March when Mack showed up at Duke's place. It was a bitterly cold day, worsened by the wind that lifted the papers along the block and sent them flying across Malcolm X Boulevard. By this time Duke had gotten used to having Kitty there and they were sitting and chatting when the door opened and Mack came in. He was on crutches.

"Well, look who's here," Duke said.

"Do you want tea?" Kitty asked.

Mack nodded and Kitty filled the kettle that Duke kept under the counter. Duke said he was going down the street to get some breakfast.

"I'll be back in an hour or so," he said, glancing at Mack.

"So what is this all about?" Mack asked when they were alone.

"I love you and I'm going to take care of you," Kitty said. "And I don't mind waiting until you let me."

"I don't need you to take care of me," Mack came back.

"Honey, you look pitiful." Kitty centered the pot on the burner.

"That's my problem," Mack said. "Not yours."

"Then how come I'm the one that's hurting so much inside?" Kitty asked him. "How come I spend so much time crying myself to sleep if it's just your problem?"

Mack was cool. He had his head to one side the way he did sometimes and narrowed his eyes. "You need to go back to school."

"Don't tell me what to do," Kitty said. "When I first told you, and everybody else in school, that I was loving you I didn't need anyone to tell me how to do it. Or didn't you notice?"

Mack sat down on one of the chairs against the wall for the customers. Kitty brought him the tea and sat next to him. He did look pitiful. His face was thin and his skin was ashy. Kitty asked him how he was doing.

"I'm getting by," he said.

"You want to go out sometime?"

"No, let me tell you what I want to do." Mack's voice rose. "I want to lead my life the way I want to lead it without you or anybody else telling me what I need to do. That's pretty clear, isn't it?"

"I guess that's supposed to chump me off, right?"

"Something like that," Mack said.

"Well, I guess it does in a way," Kitty said. "But guess what, I'm going to be here tomorrow. And I'll be waiting for you."

Kitty's eyes watered over for a minute and she wiped them quickly and then lifted her face to Mack's.

Her face, as young and brown and pretty as any Mack had ever seen, that face looking into his touched him again with its soft boldness and the eyes that searched his so intently.

Mack had a hard answer for her, but it choked him as he tried to get it out. He made a noise, something between a grunt and a croak, then stood quickly. He grabbed the crutches, knocking the teacup over.

"I'll get it," Kitty said.

Mack swung around and in a moment he was back on the block, heading for his own pad.

When Duke came back Kitty had picked up the teacup. Duke looked at her and tried to read what happened without asking. Finally his curiosity got the better of him and he did ask.

"Not much," she said softly. "Not much."

Staying out of school for a week, even two weeks, was still within the sanity range. But when a month passed and Kitty still hadn't gone to class the school began to threaten her parents. Duke knew some people on the school board and smoothed things over a bit, but he told Kitty that something had to break soon. Mack hadn't been back to the shop but a funny thing happened, people were calling him and telling him he had to do something to help Kitty. It was on the ninth of March, a Monday, when Duke and Kitty found Mack sitting on the steps of the barbershop when they arrived.

Mack was wearing an old army overcoat, and Duke noticed that he didn't have his crutches with him.

"You okay, boy?" Duke asked.

"No."

Kitty pushed in front of Duke and knelt next to Mack. "It's cold out here," she said. "Let's go inside."

Duke watched them go inside the barbershop and shook his head. He loved his granddaughter and respected her, but he was worried, more than worried, even afraid.

Inside the barbershop Kitty helped Mack to one of the barber chairs.

"Peewee called last night and said you were getting messed around over this thing and needed my help," Mack said.

"And you came down to help me." Kitty put her fingertips against Mack's cheek.

"I came down full of big things to say." Mack looked away. "I got this little temporary foot they give me. It's strapped onto my leg under my pants. I was going to walk in here and be the man and talk a lot of good-doing stuff to you."

"Run it, Mack," Kitty took his hand. "You talk all that good-doing stuff and I'll listen to you."

"Kitty, I fell three times on the way over here." The tears flooded from Mack's eyes onto his cheeks. "I'm being a big man trying to help you and I can't walk two lousy blocks. I can't be a man to you. I just can't. . . ."

His sobs filled the barbershop. Outside, the crosstown bus hissed past on the wet street. Earl was backing his van into a narrow parking spot, and brothers and sisters, already late for work, rushed toward the subway station on the boulevard.

"But you got here," Kitty said. "Down two lousy blocks, even though you feel like you want to give up, and even though your pride doesn't want you to give in even a little to being somebody that needs something or someone. You made it anyway. How much man does a girl need?"

"Kitty, I don't know what to do with myself."

"Me neither," Kitty said. She slipped her arm under Mack's. "I don't know what's going to happen tomorrow, but I know if we're together we're going to make something good happen. 'Cause we are two stubborn people. Now, you have to admit that, right?"

"Baby, you need a man that's . . ." Mack shook his head.

Kitty climbed up on the barber chair and put her head on his chest. "Tell me what kind of a man I need."

Mack struggled with the words and they didn't come right no matter how he turned them. Kitty curled up against him.

"Kitty, you're not even listening," Mack said.

"Yeah," Kitty answered. "Something like that."

A Christmas Story

It was rumored that Mother Fletcher was well over ninety years old. She had become a legend on 145th Street. If anybody wanted to know what the neighborhood looked like in the twenties, where Jack Johnson had lived, perhaps, or where James Baldwin's father had preached, Mother Fletcher could tell you. Patrolman William Michael O'Brien had heard about her shortly after his assignment to the precinct, but it wasn't until nearly three months later that he actually met the old woman.

He was on foot patrol and had stopped to pass a few words with one of the local shopkeepers when a young black girl came running up to him and told him that Mother Fletcher was sick and needed an ambulance. O'Brien knew that in this neighborhood it was nearly impossible to get a doctor who would make house calls.

But he had also been told that sometimes the people used ambulances just to go downtown.

He followed the girl into one of the buildings and into a first-floor apartment. The place was small but spotless. The floor was covered with a linoleum rug that was worn through in several spots. The porcelain in the kitchen sink was discolored but the brass fixtures were shining brightly.

"She's in here," the girl said, and went into the adjoining room.

Mother Fletcher sat upright in the white-sheeted bed, her pale green housecoat pinned at the neck. O'Brien had never seen as black a person in his entire life. Her skin was a dull ebony that seemed almost purple in the light of the lamp by her bed.

Her gray hair, still streaked with wisps of black and thinner on the sides than on the top, framed her face and, catching the light, made her look like a black version of a painted medieval saint. She was a small person, in the delicate way that a child is small, but with the quiet grace of her years. But what stood out most on the old woman were her eyes.

They were, if it was possible, even darker than her skin. Black shiny eyes that darted brightly about, checking the room for anything that might have been out of place.

"Didn't my great-great-grandchild there tell you I was sick?" Mother Fletcher shot a glance in the direction of the girl. "I gave her a dime to tell you."

"I mean," O'Brien said, "what *exactly* is the matter?"

"How do I know? I'm not a doctor." Mother Fletcher pulled the housecoat tighter around her thin shoulders.

"What's your name, please?"

"Mother Fletcher."

"What's your first name?"

"I'm Mother Fletcher, that's all. Now, are you going to get me an ambulance or do I have to send that child out for another officer?"

"We can't just call an ambulance any time someone says to call one," O'Brien said.

"Boy, I am not someone," the old woman said. "I am Mother Fletcher and you can call for an ambulance. You know how to use that radio you got."

"What is your age?" O'Brien flipped out his radio and called the emergency network.

"Full-grown," came the flat reply.

O'Brien stepped into the next room and told the operator what he had. The ambulance arrived some fifteen minutes later. Two slim attendants carried the old woman out. O'Brien wrote up the incident in his book and promptly put it out of his mind. A week later he was called into one of the precinct offices, where a lieutenant and two patrolmen were waiting for him.

"O'Brien." Lt. Stanton rolled a cigar from one side of his mouth to the other. "What's this I hear about you taking graft?"

"I don't know what you're talking about," O'Brien answered.

"Well, this package just came in from someone on your beat and it's addressed to your shield number." The lieutenant was enjoying this. "Looks like graft to me, O'Brien. Open it up."

O'Brien looked at the childish scrawl on the top of the box. *To Officer 4566.* There was no return address. He flipped open the flimsy box and took out the contents. It was a knitted green cardigan. Instead of a brand name on the label it simply repeated his badge number, 4566. O'Brien tried it on and was surprised to discover that it fit even his long arms.

"I wonder who it's from?"

"Mother Fletcher," the lieutenant said. "You do anything for her?"

"Mother Fletcher? Oh, yes, the old black lady. I called an ambulance for her. No big thing."

"She probably started making that sweater for you on the way to the hospital," Lt. Stanton said. "We had another guy here about two years ago that straightened out a hassle she had with her landlord. She made him a sweater, too. Then she decided that the landlord was right after all and she made *him* a sweater. I guess it makes her feel good. You can put a couple of bucks in the precinct fund to make up for the sweater. And don't forget to go around and thank Mother Fletcher. It's good for community P.R."

O'Brien got around to thanking the old woman a few days later, telling her how his wife had been jealous of such a fine sweater. Three weeks later another package arrived at the station house. It was a sweater for his wife. When he went over to thank Mother Fletcher for the second sweater he was careful not to mention that he had a six-year-old daughter.

Over the next months O'Brien learned more about Mother Fletcher from people on his beat. Some stories were a bit far-fetched, but they were all told in a way that said that people loved the old woman. She did her own shopping, always carrying the same blue cloth shopping bag, and always walking on the sunny side of the street "to keep the bones warm." Once O'Brien met her on the corner of 147th Street and asked her how she was feeling.

"I'm feeling just fine. I'm not cutting the rug," she said, "but I'm not lying on it, either."

O'Brien talked to her now and again when he saw her on the street, and started writing down everything she said, trying to piece together enough information to determine her true age. In truth, Mother Fletcher was the only one in his precinct that he thought of during his off-duty hours. The struggle and hassles of Harlem were not what he wanted to bring home with him. It didn't take O'Brien long to subscribe to the precinct motto— Eight and Straight. Eight hours on the job and straight out of the neighborhood.

To O'Brien, "out of the neighborhood" meant home to a ranch-style house in suburban Staten Island. He looked forward to the day when his wife, Kathy, could quit her job with the utility company and stay home with their daughter, Meaghan. He had told Kathy about Mother Fletcher and they had gone over his notes in the evenings trying to figure her age. Beyond this O'Brien was careful to keep his job apart from his family. At least he was until just before Christmas.

"Hi, honey," Bill called out as he ducked in from the light snow.

"Dinner's almost ready," Kathy answered as she came from the kitchen. "Did you ask Mother Fletcher if she remembered when Woodrow Wilson was elected President?"

"Yep."

"Well, what did she say?" Kathy wiped her hands on her apron.

"She said she remembered it."

"Did she remember how old she was then?"

"Nope, unless you can figure out how old ' 'bout half grown' is," Bill said. He tousled his daughter's hair and sat on the couch.

"What else did she say?" Kathy folded one leg under herself and sat on it.

"Not much. I think she knows that I'm trying to figure out her age and she's playing with me." Bill glanced toward the kitchen and sniffed the air. "Is that roast beef?"

"Chicken," Kathy answered. "So that's all she said today?"

"No, she complained about how loud the teenagers play their radios and, oh, yes, she invited us to Christmas dinner."

"Who invited us to dinner?" Meaghan looked up from her book.

"A lady Daddy knows in Harlem, sweetheart."

"Can we take presents over?"

"We won't be going over," Bill said.

"Why, Daddy?"

"We have other plans. We're going to . . . what are we doing for Christmas, Kathy?"

"Nothing."

"Then we can go!" Meaghan said.

"Kathy, will you deal with your daughter?" Bill smiled as he reached for the paper. "She's too much for me."

"No, I won't." Kathy got up. "I'm going to start serving dinner. And Meaghan has a right to ask a question."

"Hey, let's not make an issue of this," Bill said.

"She just asked for a simple explanation, Bill." Kathy was annoyed.

"The lady is a little different, that's all." Bill spoke to his daughter. "The place she lives in isn't very nice and Daddy would rather not spend his Christmas in that kind of a neighborhood."

"Is she a poor lady?"

"Yes, she's a poor lady."

"Then we can take her a present because poor people like presents."

"We'll send her a present if you want, Meaghan." Bill rose from the couch and went into the living room, snapping on the television before sitting down. Kathy followed him in.

"I don't like the idea of being made out to be a bad guy, Kathy," Bill said without looking away from the six o'clock news. "One word from you could have helped that little situation in there."

"Why didn't you just give her the same answer you gave Mother Fletcher? What did you tell her?"

"There are times, Kathy, when you don't give direct answers to questions. It's a way of dealing with people.

You don't reject them and you don't get yourself involved in a whole scene. Like this one, I might add."

"Would you mind giving *me* a direct answer? What did you tell her?"

"I told her yes, we'd come. But they know we don't come into that neighborhood when we're off duty," Bill answered. "And they're not that anxious to have us come, either."

"You said yes? That you'd come?" Kathy pulled her glasses from the top of her head and put them on. "That's your way of not answering a question directly?"

"I'll send her a present."

"That's awfully sweet of you, Mr. O'Brien." Kathy went back to the kitchen.

Bill turned up the television and watched as some senator complained about the military budget. If his wife had chosen this occasion to have one of her special "I simply don't understand" periods he wasn't going to fight her.

He also heard snatches of the conversation drifting from the kitchen. Meaghan was talking about getting a kitten and was trying to decide between a calico and a tabby. At any rate she seemed to have forgotten Mother Fletcher. He only hoped that Kathy would, too.

And apparently she had. For that was the last O'Brien heard about visiting the old woman. That is, it was the last thing until just after eleven on Christmas morning. He was sitting in his favorite armchair, feeling especially regal in the smoking jacket that Kathy had given him, watching a college football game, when Kathy and Meaghan came into the room with their coats on.

"Going for a walk?" Bill asked, hoping he wouldn't be expected to leave his comfortable spot.

"We're going to Mother Fletcher's for dinner," Meaghan said brightly.

"You're not going to Mother Fletcher's, Kathy. And that's that!"

"Well, then I suggest you arrest me, Mr. O'Brien." The sunlight through the window caught the flare in Kathy's eyes. "Because that will be the only way you're going to prevent our going."

"I brought her a scarf." Meaghan held a small square package.

"What is this all about?" Bill felt his face getting red. "You don't even know this woman. Why do you have to drag Meaghan all the way to Harlem?"

"I'm not dragging her anywhere. I'm giving her the present of a visit to an old lady that even you like. Now, from what you say, all I have to do is to go over to the neighborhood and ask anyone where she lives because they all know, right? Or would you like to drop us off?"

The silence of the long drive was broken only by an occasional observation from Meaghan. O'Brien took his wife slowly, carefully, through the worst streets he could find until he finally pulled up in front of Mother Fletcher's place.

"Well, well, well!" Mother Fletcher was wearing an ankle-length green dress with a white lace collar. She wore a red and gold pin shaped like a tree. "I thought I was going to be having Christmas dinner by myself this year." Bill shot a glance in Kathy's direction as they entered the small apartment. The smell of the ham in the oven filled the room.

"Mother Fletcher, this is my wife, Kathy, and this is Meaghan."

"Well, ain't she the prettiest little thing. Look just like her mama, too. Sit on down in here while I see if I can't get something together for dinner. Did I wish you a Merry Christmas yet? Merry Christmas, children."

"Merry Christmas, and here's a present." Meaghan gave Mother Fletcher the package.

"Thank you, child," Mother Fletcher said.

"Daddy didn't want to come," Meaghan said, pulling off her coat.

"I just didn't want to put you out," Bill said quickly.

"Child, I don't blame you one bit," Mother Fletcher said. "You working here all week and then coming back on a holiday. But it's good for you to see we have holidays here, too. You see the people in the street all wishing each other a Merry Christmas and dressed up in their churchgoing clothes. You see them in this frame and you get a different picture of them. Don't you think so, Officer?"

"Yeah, I guess you're right," Bill answered.

"You can take your coat off," Mother Fletcher said. "I'll put it in a safe place."

"Those plates are so lovely!" Kathy went to the kitchen table where three plates were set out. "Are they antiques?"

"Everything in this house is an antique, including me," Mother Fletcher said as she took another plate from the cabinet.

114

"It's a lovely setting and there sure are a lot of pots on the stove for you not to be expecting anyone."

"Well, honey, let me tell you something. You don't survive, and that's what I been doing all these years, you don't survive sitting around expecting folks to act right." She opened the oven door, poked a fork in the ham and watched the clear juices run down its side, and then closed it. " 'Cause the more you expect the more you get your heart broke up. But you got to be ready when they do act right because that's what makes the surviving worth surviving. That make any sense to you, honey?"

"It makes quite a bit of sense."

"That child of yours eat sweet potatoes?"

"Yes, she loves them," Kathy said. "Can I help you with anything?"

"You can help me with anything you have a mind to," Mother Fletcher said. "'Bout time you asked me, too, old as I am."

"You're not as old as Santa Claus," volunteered Meaghan.

"Santa Claus?" Mother Fletcher put down the dish towel and turned her head to one side. "Child, I knew Santa Claus when he wasn't nothing but a little fellow. Let's see now. He wasn't any bigger than you when I knew him. Me and him used to play catch down near the school yard."

And Mother Fletcher went off into telling stories to Meaghan about how long she had known Santa Claus and how she used to have to lend him her handkerchief because his nose was always running.

And the Christmas dinner wasn't the best that the

O'Briens would ever have but it was far from being the worst. But then, that's not what this story is about. This story is about how a policeman's young family brought a few hours of happiness to an old woman. Or perhaps it's about how an old woman taught a young family something about sharing. Or maybe, just maybe, it is about how a six-year-old girl found the only person in the world who played catch with Santa Claus when he was a little boy, even though she was a lot older than he was.

A Story in Three Parts

Part I Doll

Big Time Henson stood on the stoop in front of 171 West 145th Street and thought about what he had to do. There were three flights to climb to Miss Pat's house. The old woman would be awake now, thinking about going shopping as she did each afternoon. She'd ask him to go with her downtown to La Marketa and he would say no, and then she would tell him about things that happened back in the day when La Marketa would be filled with fresh food just brought in to the city and fresh fish laid out neatly on beds of cracked ice.

"You could smell the spices as soon as you got off the trolley," she would say.

As soon as you got off the trolley. The nut-brown woman had probably been beautiful when she was young, Big Time thought. He imagined his great-grandmother, smartly dressed, walking through the streets of Harlem. Big Time couldn't imagine trolleys on 125th Street, but he would nod his approval and wait on the edge of his world until she had exhausted her stories and then he would ask her to lend him a few dollars.

On the way up the stairs he began to feel sick. Once he stopped and took deep breaths, trying to calm himself down, trying to get himself into the role that he had to play. It was no use. By the time he reached her floor he realized that it was too late for anything but to ask her up front for the money.

"You're looking thin," Miss Pat said. "Are you eating enough?"

"I'm eating enough," Big Time said.

"You know when you were real little they used to call you Penny." Miss Pat took Ritz crackers from the closet and put them on the table. "I don't know how you got to be called Big Time. Penny and Big Time aren't even close. I don't like nicknames anyway."

"So you think you can spare a few dollars?" Big Time wiped away a thin edge of sweat from his upper lip.

"Have I ever told you about a woman named Doll in our family history?" She sat down in front of the refrigerator, her hands folded on the edge of the table.

"Who's Doll?" he asked. He had asked. She hadn't said no.

"Doll was a slave woman," Miss Pat said. "She was on a plantation down near Montgomery. She had two children and she had a man she loved, but they weren't married because the slaves couldn't get married like the white folks could."

"You think you could lend me the money?" Waves of nausea hit him. He sucked air through his clenched teeth.

"The whites lived in the plantation house, they used to call it the Big House," Miss Pat went on. "And the coloreds lived about a quarter mile in back of the plantation house in a little row of shacks they called the Quarters. When I was a student at Talladega College, me and Edward, your great-grandfather, went over to see the plantation. You know he was a great one for studying history. Did you know that?"

"Yeah, I remember," Big Time answered. "Okay if I open the window?"

"Sure, baby, I know how the heat can get to you sometimes."

The window was already partially opened and he pulled it all the way up. In the street below some boys were playing basketball using a milk crate as a hoop. Some older men were playing dominoes. Young men stood on the corner, as they always did, watching.

"So what happened to Doll?" he said, hoping to hurry the story.

"Doll didn't live in the Quarters with the other coloreds," Miss Pat said. "She lived in a little room in back of the kitchen in the Big House. What she did was to help the master's wife around the house. And things went all right as far as it went, with Doll not being free and everything. The master was an old man and he did pretty good. They raised cotton and hogs on that plantation. You want something to eat?"

"No," Big Time said. "I'm not hungry."

119

"Then things got hard," Miss Pat went on. "I don't know why. I guess that's the way the farming business goes. And the master started selling his slaves."

"Things were hard," Big Time said. He glanced up at the square clock on the wall over the stove. It was two-thirty. Sweet Jimmy would be back from downtown with a pocketful of Dimes.

"When Doll saw he was selling his people, she went to him and begged him not to sell her," Miss Pat said. "You know, when they sold them from Alabama and they went down to Mississippi it was really hard on them. And then they would be separated from people they knew, other colored people.

"So the master promised he wouldn't sell Doll. But one day a speculator came by—you know what a specu-lator was?"

"No, look, I have to go," Big Time said, standing.

"Well, I'm sorry you couldn't spend more time with me today," Miss Pat said, folding her hands in her lap.

There was a calmness in her voice, an evenness of tone that Big Time recognized. She knew he was sick.

"Can you lend me the money?" he asked again.

"A speculator was one of those people who went from plantation to plantation looking for slaves they could buy," Miss Pat said.

Big Time sat down. Street noises drifted up from the street. The roar of buses. A fire engine's wail. Snatches of music.

"The master had sold about as many slaves as he could sell without having to shut down his farming," Miss Pat said. "And so when the speculator came by, the slaves that were left thought they were pretty safe.

"They were out in the fields working when all of a sudden a young black girl came running out across the field. 'Master is selling the children!' she shouted. Well, you can imagine what the reaction was to that. They're out in the field working and the speculator is ready to take off their children. That's how cruel slavery times were.

"The women in the field started back toward the Big House. The overseer tried to stop them. He hit at them with his whip and tried to block them but they were determined. You know, those women loved their children. Just because a person was a slave didn't mean they didn't have the same feelings as everybody else.

"Anyway, they all got to the Big House just as the speculator was putting the children on his wagon to carry them off. Oh, they begged and they pleaded and they pleaded and they begged. The children he was selling were too young to know what was going on but when they saw their mamas crying they began to cry, too. But the master wasn't listening. Now, they said he wasn't a particularly cruel man, if you can believe that, but he had just fallen on hard times and he had done what he had done and he wasn't backing up. Doll, I guess she'd be your great-great-great-grandmother, something like that, went to her mistress and begged her, knowing that another woman would understand how she felt.

"What Doll begged her to do is just to let her hold her babies in her arms once more before they went off. She knew once they went off with the speculator she wouldn't see them again. The mistress of the plantation liked Doll and said she could say good-bye to her boys but she had to do it quick because the speculator didn't have much time to waste. He was taking the children into Montgomery. The mistress told Doll that the children would all go to good homes and be raised as house servants.

"Doll thanked her mistress and took her babies into the cabin she stayed in and she hugged them boys and hugged them and kissed them and told them how much she loved them.

"After a while the speculator got itchy and said he had to move on and the mistress sent another slave woman into Doll's cabin to get the children. When the woman came out she didn't go up to the mistress but just started walking out to the fields. The mistress called to her and threatened to have her beat good but the woman didn't turn back. Finally the mistress went into Doll's cabin herself to see what was going on.

"When she got into the cabin she saw Doll was still holding the boys in her arms and rocking them. The mistress went up to Doll to tell her that she must let the children go. That's when she saw the blood."

Miss Pat got up from the table and went to the cupboard. She moved aside a box of tea bags and brought out a small purse.

"It wasn't usual for women to kill their children during slavery times," Miss Pat said. "But it happened. I think it was something that stayed on their minds a lot even when they wouldn't do it. You know, looking at your child and being filled up with love and at the same time knowing that it was going to be a slave all its life must have been so hard."

"She killed them?"

"Sometimes you got to get your freedom the best way you can," Miss Pat said.

"What happened to Doll?" Big Time said. "She get free?"

"She got whipped," Miss Pat said. "That's the story that was handed down. And you know what?"

"What?"

"Sometimes when I think about that story you know what I think about?" Miss Pat took seven dollars from the money she had and put it down in front of Big Time. "I don't think about them children dying, which is what you think I would think about. I think about how Doll must have felt being whipped. Isn't that funny? I just think about her being tied down and that overseer or whoever it was doing the whipping trying to hurt her. You think there's just so much pain you can put on a person?"

Big Time said he didn't know. He tried to think about Doll, about how she must have felt, but his thoughts had already moved away.

"I can't even imagine trolleys on 125th Street," he said, instantly recognizing the heavy awkwardness of what he was saying.

"Well, it was a long time ago," Miss Pat answered.

When Big Time reached the street a man was arguing with a policeman while a tow truck hooked up his car. Big Time watched for a long moment, then started toward the avenue. He told himself that he would have to remember the story she had told him about Doll in case she asked him again.

Part II   Sweet Jimmy

Sweet Jimmy ran his thing behind where the old bicycle shop used to be before the landlord busted it down. He always had two heavies sitting in front of the place and two pit bulls to keep the Man off his case. The Man could collar the heavies but if they did they would just let the dogs loose and the bust would be wacked out.

Big Time showed green and went past the heavies. Inside the front room a couple of dudes were watching a talk show on television.

"Yo, Sonny, what's up?"

"Ain't nothing going on," Big Time answered to his tag. "You just chilling?"

"Yeah, something like that," Fish said. "You should

check out these Snow Whites on the tube, man. They each got two boyfriends and they messing with both of them."

"That's the thing," Big Time said. "You think you're playing a babe and they're playing you."

"Word. But I wouldn't go on no television and let the world know about it, man," Fish said.

"You would if they offered you some Presidents." Big Time didn't know the other dude. "You can cop the money and then let the babes walk."

"Yeah, I hear you," Big Time said. He was feeling sick again. "Sweet Jimmy in the back?"

"Yeah."

Big Time stepped through the curtain that separated the front room from the back. It was dark and he stood in the doorway trying to get his eyes right and knowing he wouldn't. There was a radio on and somebody was flowing strong but Big Time couldn't figure out who it was.

"Yo, Sweet Jimmy, what's happening?"

"You are if you're righteous." Sweet Jimmy's voice came from the corner.

Big Time squinted and found Sweet Jimmy's shape. He went over to him and took out the small wad of bills he had counted over and over again in Miss Pat's hallway. Sweet Jimmy looked at the bills, counted them out, then threw them into a cardboard box.

Sweet Jimmy handed Big Time the syringe and said something that Big Time didn't quite catch.

What he told himself was that he was going to wait it

out. Stay away from the tracks and just skin pop. Hold off the nausea and mellow out slow. He was down with the easy way.

"You need help?"

Big Time looked up and saw the kid that Sweet Jimmy let hang around. The kid could find a vein in the dark if you needed that kind of help.

"Ain't going there," Big Time said.

He found a chair against the wall, sat down, took a deep breath, and then slid the point of the needle under the skin on the inside of his wrist. He hoped the stuff wasn't weak. Sweet Jimmy wasn't known for weak stuff. Sweet Jimmy was straight, which was why so many people turned to Sweet Jimmy when they needed to get right.

"Yo, Sonny," Sweet Jimmy called from across the room. "Are you down with the S.A.T.?"

"Yeah, I'm down," Big Time said.

"My sister is looking to take the S.A.T. again," Sweet Jimmy said. "She got to get a scholarship to get into this school she wants to make up in Boston, man."

"You can't carry the weight?" Big Time asked.

"She's doing her Snow White thing," Sweet Jimmy came back. "You know, walking away from the 'hood and the good."

"Yeah, I know what you mean." Big Time felt himself flushing, felt the drugs flooding through his body, felt himself easing into that state in which he just didn't care about anything. He relaxed into the chair that Sweet Jimmy had provided, and struggled to stay alert.

Sweet Jimmy's voice was, at the same time, bouncing around his head and coming from a distance.

"So what she's doing is running around trying to show what she's all about. The way I figure it is if the ho wants to go, let her go because I ain't running behind her. You know what I mean?"

"Yeah," Big Time answered. "You can't, you know, get to somebody when they want to be on their own."

"So I had to turn her out because I can't use nobody around that brings me down. If you bring me down I got to turn you loose because you get in the way of business. Wack don't walk and flak don't talk in no business . . ."

There was a dude sucking on a crack pipe and Big Time thought he was looking in his direction. What was he checking him out for? How come Sweet Jimmy had the guy in his place, anyway?

Big Time felt himself easing out but with the pipe sucker watching him he had to fight the nod. He had paid twenty dollars for the hit and Sweet Jimmy's stuff was correct but now he was freaking because of the guy watching him. And all the stuff about his sister might have been a trick bag. He might have been testing him, to see what he knew, if he could hold his stuff or if he was going to slip and slide so that he could be had or maybe run lame but he knew he could separate himself out from the dudes who were down and out and he knew he was dealing with the real game so nobody could work their show or creeping and peeping and waiting for you to wear down so they could get over. Big Time was tired but he still checked out the guy across from him letting the pipe fall across his lap and leaning back from his hit and he wasn't nothing but a crackhead trying to front like he was stupid clean with a gangsta lean and Sweet Jimmy's snap rap flowing all around him dissing his sister's flavor and checking him out at the same time and sleep . . . and sleep . . . and sleep. . . .

Sleep.

Wake.

"Yo, man, you got a lot on the cap," Sweet Jimmy said. "So when you see her you can tell her that you'll hook her up with the S.A.T."

"Yeah, it's no big thing."

Down from Sweet Jimmy's place a woman was bargaining with a used furniture dealer over the price of a lamp. The man, short and dark, was trying to explain that he could get fifty dollars for the lamp downtown and had to charge her twenty-five.

"This lamp doesn't even work!" the woman was saying.

"It's art deco," the dealer said. "They go for big money sometimes. Hundreds of dollars."

"Not when they don't work." The woman's voice rose in pitch and she separated her legs, securing her position on the sidewalk. "If it doesn't give out any light, what good is it?"

Big Time was tired. He checked his pockets. He had seventy-five cents left. He remembered he had a can of tuna fish at home and wondered if he really was in the mood for tuna fish. Sometimes tuna fish upset his stomach and he was already feeling a little nauseous.

Part III   The Roof

"So where were you?" his mother had asked. "If you weren't in school all last week just where were you?"

He walked out. Didn't she know there weren't any answers? What was he going to say? That he had been searching and that he didn't know what he was searching for? That he was afraid and looking for a place to be safe. That he didn't know what made him afraid?

That he was tired?

There were no answers and the questions ate at him. He walked out and started down the stairs, her voice still ringing in his ears. He stopped. Where to go? Leaning against the wall he closed his eyes and listened for the feelings that rumbled through his silence. Nausea? So soon? No, just fatigue.

He thought about the warehouse roof and started downstairs again. Sometimes, when it rained, the leftover garbage would mix with water and begin to stink. Big Time squinted into the darkness. It was growing cold but he still didn't want to go home and listen to his mother's recital of his failings. Not tonight.

Across the street and into the alley that led to the fire escape. Carefully climb the first ladder, bracing his feet on the window ledge, and then onto the iron stairway that led to the roof. There was a light coming from one window. The building was abandoned by everyone who could make a dollar on it. A few homeless people used it now, sometimes a crackhead down on his luck. Big Time slipped by the window with the light without looking in. Respect.

Too cold. He hadn't noticed how cold it had grown. If he could stand it an hour, maybe two, his mother would be asleep. He wondered what she dreamt about. Grass? Distant white clouds against a shock of blue sky? What did Miss Pat dream about? She was old enough to have a head full of movies.

He thought the boy was a dog, that is, when the boy came out of the shadow Big Time imagined that it was a small dog that had been lying in the shadows.

"Who you?" he asked, his heart calming, his breathing headed back to normal.

"Benny," the boy said.

"Penny?" Big Time asked. "Your name is Penny?"

"Benny," the boy repeated. "With a *B*."

"What you doing up here?"

"Nothing," Benny said. He stepped forward into the dim moonlight.

He was eight, maybe nine, Big Time thought. He could have been eleven if the thin arms coming from the short-sleeved and collarless shirt were from hunger. The jeans he wore were worn and dirty.

"What you mean by 'nothing'?" Big Time asked.

The boy shrugged and looked away.

Beyond the roof of the warehouse the 'hood lay in smoldering darkness, the amber lights of the sleepless glaring, forming odd patterns of bothered art. Even farther below, the streetlights marked off sullen pathways that squared back into themselves.

"You should be home," Big Time said.

"Should be."

"Where you live?"

"Malcolm X," Benny said, referring to the avenue.

"I haven't seen you around." Big Time pulled his jacket close.

"I seen you," Benny replied. "You hang on 145th."

"What you do—go around watching people?"

"Sometimes." The boy let the word dangle in the cool air.

Silence. Big Time didn't know what to say, or if he really wanted to say anything. He was sleepy, that was good. But he didn't want to sleep on the roof if the boy was there. He wondered if the boy, if Benny, felt the same way.

Music came in snatches as if the wind only carried what it chose to bring to them, brief moments of rhythm, a piece of song, a distant hint of melody. The silence fit in well.

BLOOF!

Benny jumped and Big Time whirled toward the door to the stairway.

"What was that?" Benny asked.

"Nothing," Big Time said. And then, "Probably those junkies down below."

"You come up the fire escape?" Benny asked, his voice high and still filled with tension.

"Yeah."

Benny went to the back of the building and looked down.

"There's a fire," he called back.

Big Time went to the roof edge and looked. Flames

were shooting out of the window onto the fire escape on the floor below. Now there was shouting.

"Damned crackheads must have been freebasing," Big Time said. "They started a fire."

"What we going to do?"

"Shut up, man!" Big Time felt the anger surge in him. "What you here for, anyway?"

"We gonna die?"

"I said shut up!"

Big Time went to the door leading to the stairs and tried it. It was locked. He pulled it harder. Nothing. He knew it would be nailed shut.

"You can't open the door?" Benny asked.

"Look, I don't care if we burn up or not," Big Time said. "It don't make me no never mind."

Big Time sat down on a box and crossed his legs at the ankle. He watched Benny go to the door and pull on it, his small body looking even smaller as it became more desperate. Behind him the light from the flames flickered.

It don't make me no never mind, he thought. Lie. Panic inside, like the panic of feeling sick and not having any money. A growing anxiety that already had filled him, and now threatened to overflow.

"Why don't you do something?" Benny said. "You grown!"

"That don't mean nothing when the door's locked," Big Time said.

"Yeah, it do!" There was a trace of snot under Benny's nose. "Yeah, it do."

The kid was wrong, Big Time said. Being grown

didn't mean nothing. Being grown just meant you were around for a while. All he had to do was to take a chill pill. Relax until the set was over.

The boy went to the edge of the roof and looked over again. He backed off quickly. Then he went to the front of the roof. There was no fire escape there, no way to get down. He put one leg over, as if he were going to try to climb down the front of the building, then pulled it back.

"Man, sit down," Big Time called to Benny.

The building was on the corner and one side went straight down. Big Time remembered looking at the faded sign painted on the bricks. It read SINCLAIR INKS. Big Time watched the boy look down and wondered if he would jump.

BLOOF!

The flames shot past the roof briefly and went down. They were followed by belching, choking smoke. Big Time went to the edge and looked over. The fire was coming out of two windows now.

"Help!" the boy was calling over the side.

Big Time waited. He watched Benny run from side to side. For a while the boy's panic was more interesting than the fire. What would he do? How did he feel? Did he feel alone even though he, Big Time, was still there? Could somebody be alone with another person so close?

Benny was crying as the flames burned the edge of the roof. There was a small wall, less than three feet high, on the sides of the building. Benny went to the other side of the roof and looked over. Then he ran back to the center and ran toward the edge, stopping when he reached the wall. He had lost his nerve.

You grown, he had said.

What could he do? Doors locked. Fire coming. He wished he had a hit. What he needed was a hit.

"You got any weed?" he asked Benny.

"I don't smoke," Benny said.

Big Time had to pee. He went to a side of the roof and started peeing. Behind him Benny was shouting off the edge of the roof. He was calling out "Help!" into the darkness.

He was scared but it wasn't a big thing. He had been there before. Only thing that could happen was him and the boy going down. It wouldn't even make the news. Two dudes from the 'hood found dead. That wasn't even news.

"I'm going to try to jump to the other building," Benny said, his eyes searching Big Time's face.

Big Time walked slowly to the edge of the roof. He looked over. It was a good eight feet across to the next building and maybe a yard down. It was too far to jump if he tried going over the wall. And there was no way the kid could make it.

"We're trapped, man." Benny's face was tear-streaked as he sided closer against Big Time.

"I'm not trapped," Big Time said.

"You going to jump?" Benny asked.

Why don't you do something? You grown!

"What you so scared for?" Big Time asked. "Being scared's not going to help you get off the roof."

"What you going to do?" Benny insisted.

A hit would have mellowed things out, Big Time

knew, but he also knew that mellowing out would kill him. He had always known that.

The smoke was getting thicker and flames were rising above the edge of the roof. Nausea. His eyes were stinging, his hands were shaking. He wanted to sit down and go to sleep.

"What you going to do, man?" Benny asked again.

"Take it easy," Big Time said. He looked over the small wall. There were a few bricks protruding from the wall. He stood and put one leg over, found a brick that stuck out an inch from the wall and tested his weight on it.

"You going to jump?" Benny's face was full of fear.

"I don't know," Big Time said. He swung his other leg over until he was sitting on the small wall with his legs dangling. "Sit up here with me, Benny."

"I can't, I'm scared."

"Yo, man, I'm scared, too. Hey, ain't that something. I'm sitting up here on the wall and I'm scared out my damned mind."

"Why you laughing if you scared?" Benny asked. "Why you laughing?"

"'Cause I didn't know how scared I was before," Big Time said. "Now I do. Now I know just how I feel. C'mon, the fire's getting closer."

"I'm too scared." Benny took a step back.

"Hey, I'm grown, Benny," Big Time said. "I know what I'm doing. Take my hand. It's okay. Really."

Flames, like yellow demons, streaked through the thick smoke that poured from the fire. Benny started to choke, his chest heaving up and down with his coughing. They heard the sound of fire engines and Big Time looked down to see a fire truck go up Amsterdam Avenue.

"They don't know about this fire yet," Big Time said. "We've got to bust a move. Come on, take my hand. We'll jump to the next roof."

"We can't make it," Benny answered. "It's too far."

"It's not the best way to get down," Big Time said. "But it's what we got."

The fire crackled and a shower of cinders came from one corner. Benny, his teeth clenched, climbed onto the small wall.

"We can't make it," he whispered.

We can't make it, Big Time thought. He could fling the kid, though. If the kid wouldn't hold on to him he could fling the kid onto the roof.

"Get ready," Big Time said quietly.

Benny held Big Time's arm and Big Time pushed him roughly away. "Don't punk out on me," he said. "Don't be grabbing me, just jump when I tell you."

"I can't." Benny looked back toward the burning roof. "I just . . ."

"*Jump!*" Big Time leaned forward into the dark space, felt his feet against the wall and pushed as hard as he could, flinging Benny into the blackness in front of him.

For an eternity they hung in space, screaming and straining and reaching for something to catch on to. Big Time felt his chest hit the edge of the other roof and his legs go over the side. He was sliding over, he grabbed something, a bottle, it moved and he grabbed the edge of a vent.

"Benny!"

"I'm okay," came the reply.

"I'm hanging over the edge," Big Time said.

"I'll go get some help," Benny said.

No, don't go. Please, don't go. How long could he hang on? His chest was hurting, and his knees. He tried pulling himself up and felt a sharp pain in his wrist. He was scared and hurting and desperate and it felt good. He thought he was going to laugh again. He imagined himself falling off the roof, falling backward to a sure dying and laughing all the way. He hung on and lifted his leg. The knee throbbed, the leg hurt, but he got his foot up on the roof. He pulled as slowly as he could. He didn't want to die. He pulled himself until he got his shoulders up and was able to roll his body to safety.

The smell of tar was sweet. He could see his wrist. It was bleeding. Everything was sore. His body shook with hurt and fatigue. He stood up just as the door opened and Benny came running through.

"You made it!"

"Yeah."

"You were hanging off the roof?" A heavyset woman stood in the doorway behind Benny. "That's what the boy said."

"Yeah," Big Time said. "I'm okay now."

"Lord, look at that building burning," the woman said. "Must be those junkies that hang out over there."

"Yeah," Big Time said.

Benny was talking about the fire as they went down

the stairs. It had already passed over into adventure for the boy. By the time they reached the first floor there were fire engines out front and a small knot of people, only half-interested in the fire, watched the firemen work.

"I'll see you around the block," Big Time said. "And the next time you see me you better say hello or something."

"Yeah, I will," Benny said.

By the time he got home he was getting stiff from the bruises. He knew it would be worse in the morning. He thought about Benny again. The next time he saw him maybe he would even hang out with him a taste, rap to him about staying away from the roof, getting home early, and other good-doing stuff. Maybe.

Block Party—
145th Street Style

"He said *what*?" Peaches looked up from the math book we were studying from.

I've known Peaches all my life, which means for fifteen years, and I hated to see her sad. Peaches is not the kind of girl to get messed around easy but I was there when her mama told her about Big Joe.

"He asked me to set a date to marry him," Sadie Jones said, standing at the sink.

"He's got some nerve," Peaches said. She took a deep breath and shook her head.

"And I told him I would," her mama said. "Honey, it's time I got married. I'm not getting any younger and you know Joe's really sweet."

Peaches didn't say another word but in a minute I could see the tears running down her face. When her mama came over and put her arm around her shoulders

Peaches shrugged her off. Later, when we were checking out the tube, I asked her why she was so upset about Big Joe.

"You know your mama likes him and he's sweet for an Old School dude," I said.

"It doesn't have anything to do with Big Joe, Squeezie," Peaches said later, tagging me like she always does when she's upset. "I think if she loved my daddy she wouldn't go messing around with somebody else."

I wasn't even going there. I mean, you're supposed to give people their propers when they're alive but after they're gone for years all you have to do is just don't diss them. I personally never diss no dead people, anyway. Okay, so Peaches was sad and walking around like she lost her best friend, which is me. The closer the wedding got the more down she was. Nothing anybody said could cheer her up. Her mama asked her up front if she wanted her to say no to Big Joe.

"Honey, I'll do it for you," Peaches' mama said.

"Do what you want," Peaches said.

I thought that was kind of mean but I knew my friend was hurting inside. She was only nine when her father passed but they had been real close. She always said that he had been her best friend before me. When Peaches was young he used to take her to the park and he would get right down in the sandbox and make castles and stuff with her. When we got older he would take me and Peaches to a restaurant on Saturday afternoons and make believe we were grown ladies and that was, like, super-cool. Having your father for a best friend was all right and I could see how she felt. But I could also see her mother's point of view. Big Joe had loved her mama for a long time and he did own a Bar-B-Que joint that was the serious bomb. What's more, it didn't take geometry or nothing like that to see that her mama loved Big Joe, too.

When the woman who's the borough president announced that the city was sponsoring a street fair on 145th Street, I saw a chance to cheer Peaches up. Peaches and me are home girls and I can't stand for her to be sad all the time.

"So let's go on to the street fair and eat some potato salad or whatever else they got," I said.

She said okay and I said we should wear our black pants and put on some fly tops in case any boys showed and she said she wasn't in the mood for boys and she was going to wear the top she had on. Whatever.

So we're at the street fair and it looks like it could develop into something. They had hooked up some monster amps on a flatbed truck and the usual hoochie mamas were showing off their stuff. Me and Peaches, who are both on a conservative tip, were standing in front of my crib checking things out. I'm not homely but I don't have Peaches' looks so I was scopin' and hopin', if you know what I mean.

Leroy hooked up some jams and the dancing started. I was wishing that somebody would come over to us because I knew Peaches loved to dance and I figured that maybe a little shaking would get her out of her bad mood. That's when J.T. showed up.

J.T. was tall and dark, had pretty eyes, a thin face, and he was built nice for a sixteen-year-old. The guys on the block said he could really play ball, too. But he was always in trouble. He had even been in the Juvenile Detention Facility last Christmas for snatching a white lady's pocketbook. You knew you were going to read about him in the newspaper one day or see his picture on television with his hands behind his back.

"Hey, Squeeze, what's happening?" he said.

"Hey, J.T.," I came back.

He stood a little way from us and started eyeballing the food table. There was beans and rice, fried chicken, ribs, plantains, and corn on the cob.

I pointed him out to Peaches and right away she got caught up in her attitude and talking about why J.T. had to come around to mess things up.

"It's a street fair and he lives on this street," I said.

"You know he's a thief, right?" Peaches said. "And I got the money on me for the wedding gift."

Peaches and me had gone downtown earlier looking for a wedding gift for her moms and Big Joe.

"Why are you going to spend two hundred dollars if you're so messed around about the marriage?" I had asked her when we were walking out of Macy's.

"I got to get them something," she said. "And I am not messed around about the marriage!"

Whatever. Anyway, J.T. was slowly sliding over toward the eats.

"What do you want?" Peaches asked him.

"This is a free party, right?" he said.

"So you coming around to cop what you can get for free?" Peaches asked in this nasty way.

I didn't want to get into nothing with J.T., because sometimes when boys go to those youth houses they come out dangerous, so I told Peaches to cool it.

"Cool *what*?" Peaches put her hand on her hip. "I'm not scared of no J.T."

"Why don't you just chill?" J.T. said.

"Why don't you just shut up?" Peaches got right up in J.T.'s face. "You shouldn't even be talking to decent people. I know you're sleeping in the street. You ain't even got a home and you're telling somebody to chill. Leave me alone!"

Peaches was getting loud, flashing proud and drawing a crowd. People were turning to see what was going on. Mrs. Liburd, a little Bajun lady, came over and said we shouldn't argue.

"You're such lovely children," she said, reminding us that we didn't need to be showing ourselves out.

J.T. dropped his head and walked away. He went toward where I thought he lived. You could see the hurt in his eyes. It made me feel bad for him and for Peaches, too, because that's not the way she shows when things go right.

I thought about saying something to Peaches but I figured it wasn't the right time.

Some brothers with dreads started playing steel drums and that was getting us back to a good mood. The steel drums were on the money and when Big Joe showed up with a portable barbecue grill everything was everything. Peaches' mom was working with Big Joe and they looked like a cool couple.

"You want to go help them serve?" I asked Peaches.

"They didn't ask me to help them," Peaches said.

"Maybe because they're afraid you're going to chump them off," I said. "Like you did J.T."

"They just don't need me," Peaches said. "I usually make the potato salad at home. Now she got him I guess she wants to eat his nasty potato salad."

I have eaten girlfriend's potato salad and it's not all that but I saved that for later. I went over myself to lend a hand.

Big Joe had on his chef hat and an apron. He was slicing up the ribs and dipping them in the sauce. Peaches' mama had on an apron and she was serving up some lemonade. Every once in a while she would glance over at Big Joe and give him a little smile and he would give her a little smile right back. I like to see that in old folks.

Me and Peaches have been best friends for as long as I can remember but wrong is wrong and everybody knows what God don't like. After a while Peaches did come over but she made sure nobody thought she was having a good time.

"Hold up on the serving until we set out the trash cans," Big Joe said.

Big Joe was a real good cook and the food line was stretched halfway down the block.

"Now hear this! Now hear this!" It was Leroy on the P.A. system. "Anybody who is already fat and greasy should get on the back of the line and please save me some food if y'all want me to play some decent music!"

With the food going, the music blowing, 145th Street was like a huge rent party without the door charge. Everybody was having fun. Except for Peaches, of course, but you could see she was needing to work at being miserable. Then little Debbie, wearing a dress so tight you could see everything she had, said something to the guys in the steel band and they started playing a reggae version of "Here Comes the Bride," which was corny but in an okay kind of way.

Peaches smiled and I half smiled back at her.

"You still mad at me, girlfriend?" she asked.

"No," I said, even though I was, a little.

"Look, you want to come with me and I'll take a plate up to J.T.?" she said. "I know I didn't act right."

"You don't have to do that," I said. "Just let it slide."

"Right, so now J.T.'s mad at me, and I hurt my moms, and now my main girl is hurt, too." Peaches gave me that smile she knows always gets around me.

"You know you got a fast mouth, girl," I said. "I don't know how you can be so correct and righteous in your heart, and still fix your mouth to say all them mean things."

"As long as I got my Squeezie to get me straight I'm all right," Peaches said. "Come on upstairs with me."

I really didn't want to go up to where J.T. was. I was just happy that girlfriend was seeing where she was at. "I'm not going up there," I said, but when she fixed a plate of chicken and greens and salad and said she was going anyway I naturally had to go with her.

We covered the plate with some aluminum foil and

went into the building next to John's Fish House. The halls were kind of dim and the tin on the stairs rattled as we went up, Peaches going first and me behind her.

"I guess I got to get used to my mama getting married, Squeezie," Peaches said.

"I think you do," I said. "Same way she got to get used to it if you get married."

"She's still wrong for marrying him so soon," Peaches said.

We went up to the top floor to where we thought J.T. lived and saw there was a padlock on the door. Peaches turned and looked at me and I looked at her.

"Maybe they moved," I said.

We went back toward the stairs and Peaches stopped. She looked up past the landing that led to the roof. Then she started up even though there wasn't much light up there. Like a good homey I followed.

"Who coming up here!" The voice sounded like a growl more than a person and I was ready for some serious stepping.

"It's me," Peaches said. "That you, J.T.?"

"Get out of here!" J.T. stepped down in front of Peaches. He had his shirt off and he spread his legs and had his fists balled up.

"We brought you a plate," Peaches said.

Wham! J.T. knocked that plate from Peaches' hand and it went up against the wall.

"What's wrong with you, fool?" Peaches was up in his face again.

"Get out of here!" he said.

I was reaching for Peaches to pull her back because I

didn't want her to get hurt. Peaches came down two steps and turned back toward J.T. He was so mad the spit was flying out with his words.

Then, just when I thought we were going to go on down and get back to the block party, Peaches started back up the stairs again. J.T. put his arm in front of her and Peaches grabbed it and started wrestling with him.

"Don't you touch her!" I heard myself screaming.

J.T. slipped on the stairs and somehow Peaches pushed him down a little and ran past him up toward the roof. Something inside me just went crazy, like a heavy panic thing, and I tried to run up the stairs after her and J.T. put his hand right over my face and started pushing me back. I hit the wall and had to catch myself before I fell down the stairs. Then J.T. turned to go after Peaches. I caught his leg and he kicked me with his other leg and I had to let him go.

So by this time I'm crying and my shoulder is hurt. Then I hear J.T. cursing again, and this time it's cursing and almost the same growling noise he was making before. If it had been anybody else but Peaches, I would have been down the stairs in a heartbeat, but I couldn't leave her in no danger.

I got my teeth clenched up and went upstairs ready to scratch J.T.'s eyes clean out of his head if I had to. He was standing on the steps just below the door that led to the roof. He saw me and tried to push me back with one hand.

"Just get out of here! Just get out of here!" he was saying.

I looked on the landing and Peaches was down on her knees and there was somebody else there, too. It was J.T.'s mama. She was sitting on the landing with a blanket around her. There was an empty cracker box, old newspapers, and open cans of food scattered around the landing.

J.T.'s mama was shivering. The light coming through a crack in the door to the roof filtered through her hair to make a halo around her thin face. She looked over Peaches' shoulder to me, the big sad dark eyes looking like they were a hundred years old. Peaches was just holding her with both arms.

J.T. was still carrying on but he was slowing down and the growling noise was like him halfway crying at the same time he was talking. After a while he stopped and leaned against the banister. His mama brought her hand out from the blanket around her and she put it on Peaches' arm.

"Squeezie, go downstairs and tell Big Joe to come up," Peaches said, softly.

"I don't need no Big Joe up here," J.T. said.

"Tell him that I need him to come up here," Peaches said. There were tears coming down her face. "Tell him that I need him real bad."

I went downstairs slow and realized that my leg was hurt, too, as well as my shoulder. The music was still going on when I reached the street and it took me a while to get through the crowd and get to where Big Joe and Peaches' mama were.

"Squeezie, what's wrong, baby?" Peaches' mama said.

I tried to say it without crying but I couldn't and I could see Mrs. Jones getting more and more upset.

"Is Peaches hurt?" Big Joe asked.

"No, she just needs to help J.T.'s mama, I think," I said.

"We can take care of it," Big Joe said. He was calm as he took off his apron. "We can take care of it."

We went upstairs, and Peaches' mama wanted to run up, but Big Joe kept saying everything was all right and we went slow with him leading the way. When we got up to the top of the stairs, J.T. was sitting with his head in his hands. Big Joe told him to move and J.T. slid over.

Peaches was still sitting with J.T.'s mama, kind of rocking her in her arms. After making sure that Peaches was okay, Mrs. Jones helped J.T.'s mama to stand up and Big Joe carried her in his arms all the way downstairs and up the street to Mother Fletcher's house.

J.T. had come down and he hung back, watching. Peaches went toward him and I went over in case some fighting was going to break out but she just took his hand. She didn't say nothing, just took his hand like she was there for him.

"I couldn't even do nothing for my own mother," J.T. said. He had tears running down his cheeks. "I feel bad about, you know, fighting you and everything."

"This is 145th Street," Peaches said. "Hurt happens here just like everywhere else. Sometimes you can deal with it, sometimes you just got to get some help."

J.T. and his mama stayed with Mother Fletcher for a

few days and then Big Joe got them a little place on 141st Street, across from the school. It wasn't no mansion but it was cool. Then Peaches gave them her whole two hundred dollars wedding gift money, which J.T. said he was going to pay back but I know he didn't have a job. I wouldn't have given anybody *all* my money. But Peaches got that kind of big heart in her. And that's how the whole block is, in a way. Yeah, you got some people who do ugly things, but I think, mostly, if they had a good chance they would be okay.

The next month was the wedding and it turned out so good! Peaches' mama had her hair done real nice, up off her neck, and she was so beautiful that I cried, which was no big thing because I always cry at weddings. Then Peaches, Big Joe, and Sadie had them a family hug which got my boo-hooing into high gear again.

"I'm still a little scared about Mama getting married," Peaches said afterward.

"But we'll deal with it, right?" I said.

"Yeah, Squeezie," she said, "we can deal with it."

"You're still number one with me," I said.

"I'm still *numero uno* with my mama, too," Peaches said. "Big Joe can't compete with me."

"Go on, girlfriend."

So that was what happened to Peaches and her mama, and to J.T. and his mama. We still see J.T. and his mama around. They're not really kicking it too tough right now but they're sliding by, you know, staying strong and being righteous. I know they're going to make it.

Oh yeah, what we gave Big Joe and the new Mrs. Big

Joe for a wedding gift was a pair of boss imitation Tiffany lamps that cost sixty-three dollars. All the money came from me but that was all right because, like I always say, me and Peaches got a friendship that's all that and then some. You know what I mean?

WALTER DEAN MYERS TALKS ABOUT WRITING *145TH STREET*

Question: Why does Harlem figure so prominently in your work?

Walter Dean Myers: In a conversation with the novelist James Baldwin, we discussed growing up in Harlem and our mutual love for books. When I told Mr. Baldwin how I almost turned away from writing because the books I was reading did not reflect my African American heritage or home, he said he had felt the same way. His response was to leave Harlem and make a new life in Europe. I left the meeting thrilled that I had had the opportunity to chat with someone I considered a hero, but I quickly realized how much more the conversation would have helped me at fourteen. I became determined to write about Harlem, and to include the lives that were missing from the wonderful books I had read.

Q: Why did you choose 145th Street for the setting of this short-story collection?

WDM: I grew up on Morningside Avenue. I thought people might not instantly recognize that wide street as being part of Harlem, so I chose 145th Street, where I often hung out with friends.

Q: Most of your books are novels. Why did you write *145th Street* as short stories?

WDM: I wanted to include a large array of characters, so I chose the short-story format instead of a novel. That way

I could use many of the people I knew (as I always do)—I had photos of many of them. I put the photos on a large sheet of poster board, which I mounted on the wall behind my computer. It was fun to sit at the computer every day and write about people I knew. When the book came out, some of them recognized themselves as characters in the stories. They were surprised that I knew so much about them. I'm a very good listener!

Q: What's different about writing short stories compared to writing a novel?

WDM: I like writing short stories because I enjoy the challenge of expanding one character and one incident into a meaningful slice of life as well as a reflection of who I am.

Q: Has the real 145th Street changed since you wrote these stories?

WDM: All of Harlem is changing these days, but it has changed before and, in my mind, still remains a wonderful place.

Q: You served as the 2012–2013 National Ambassador for Young People's Literature. Your platform was "Reading is not optional." What did you learn from your travels as ambassador?

WDM: The skills you need to survive are changing. Today's young people need excellent reading skills to move ahead with their lives. Just getting by doesn't get you by anymore. Oddly, the emphasis on education that I experienced is not as widespread. There are still great schools and great students, but too many young people seem to be alienated from both school and society. We need to turn this around.

CELEBRATING

WALTER DEAN MYERS

TRIBUTES FROM:

Christopher Myers

Michael Cart

Deborah Taylor

Lois Lowry

Claudette S. McLinn

Natasha Díaz

Pauletta Brown Bracy

Cicely Lewis

Renée Watson

Rudine Sims Bishop

Jason Reynolds

Nic Stone

CHRISTOPHER MYERS

I remember once—it was in Brooklyn—we went to a high
    school.
And a kid looked at you and said,
"So you supposed to be a famous writer?"
And you said something like,
"Well, I'm kind of well known."
And then he said, "But you look like an old dude from my
    block, like a regular person."

We went for a walk after that, through one of those parts of
    Red Hook
Made of chain-link and brick towers, the kind of place we
    feel at home.
And you smiled, and you said, "I think I got through to that
    one."

Meaning that maybe he got that key that took you from the
    George Bruce Library on 125th Street, through
    hundreds of books and poems and stories.
That maybe he understood that yes,
We are bound by the stories that are told about us,
But we too can write our stories.

And in that sense of giving someone a tomorrow,
You said, "I think I did good."

Dad, I think you did good too.
We all do.

Love,
Chris

Christopher Myers is a widely acclaimed author and illustrator, as well as the Creative Director of the Random House Children's Books imprint Make Me a World. His fine art has been exhibited at MoMA PS1 and other museums and galleries nationally and internationally. In addition to illustrating his own titles, Myers has worked with numerous authors, including E. E. Cummings, Zora Neale Hurston, and his father, Walter Dean Myers. Christopher and his father worked together on the Caldecott Honor winner Harlem, *as well as the Coretta Scott King Honor–winning books* Black Cat *and* H.O.R.S.E.

The following is an excerpt from Christopher Myers' speech at the 2019 American Library Association's Annual Conference & Exhibitions in Washington, DC. Christopher Myers accepted the 2019 Children's Literature Legacy Award on behalf of his late father, Walter Dean Myers.

MICHAEL CART

Walter Dean Myers is a giant of young adult literature, one of the most important writers to enrich and honor the field with his work. Acknowledging this was the 1994 presentation to him of the prestigious Margaret A. Edwards Award for lifetime achievement in young adult literature. This was only one of the many honors, accolades, and awards he received, however; notable among the rest were the first Michael L. Printz Award for his searing novel *Monster*; five Coretta Scott King Awards; two Newbery Honor Medals; and, most recently, the Children's Literature Legacy Award, which acknowledges his "vast literary talent and deep empathy."

Writing for younger readers as well as young adults, he created, over the course of his fifty-year career, more than one hundred books in a wide variety of forms and formats, including novels, short story collections, picture books, and nonfiction. In each of these he succeeded brilliantly at an urgent task: giving faces to young people of color, young people who had been invisible in books for far too long. "What I can do," he said in his Edwards Award acceptance speech, "is help make all our children and all our young adults visible again. I can help begin the process of peeling away labels they have been burdened with that diminish their humanity." He did this by bringing them to vibrant, individual life, as he demonstrated in this collection of extraordinary, timeless stories. Taking place in his signature neighborhood of 145th Street, the stories are notable for their beautifully realized setting, of course, but also for their universality. In his telling, a single street becomes a whole world of wisdom. Like all of his books, the stories are tough and tender, gritty and graceful, humorous and serious. They epitomize the larger body of his work, of which he once said, "If we do not write about all our children, write about them with hard truths and a harder compassion, then we have, in a very significant way, failed our own futures."

An avid reader as a youth who found solace in books, he grew up to understand the power of reading, which he championed as the National Ambassador for Young People's Literature when he chose as his theme "Reading Is Not Optional." Reading is instead, as he demonstrated, imperative, with its capacity to change and even save lives, as all of his books do with such honesty, integrity, and empathy. In sum, Walter Dean Myers is truly sui generis, one of a kind.

Reflecting on his legacy, he once wrote, "I would like to be remembered as giving something back to the world." There is absolutely no question that he will be.

A columnist and reviewer for Booklist *magazine, Michael Cart, a past president of the Young Adult Library Services Association, is the author or editor of twenty-three books, including the young adult novel* My Father's Scar.

DEBORAH TAYLOR

Like many others, I first connected with Walter Dean Myers through a book. I had been a young adult librarian for just over a year when *Fast Sam, Cool Clyde, and Stuff* was published. I was always looking for books that I could take with me into schools and "book talk." The titles that resonated with the teens in my inner-city Baltimore neighborhood needed drama and characters that intrigued the students. *Fast Sam, Cool Clyde, and Stuff* had both, as well as a special dollop of humor. Walter created a loving portrayal of young people who had their share of issues but who were so much more than their circumstances. As Walter continued to provide us with rich and varied stories in a range of formats and genres, his popularity with the teens in my community grew. When they read a book like the Newbery Honor–winning *Scorpions*, they understood that Mr. Myers was a writer who knew the challenges they faced. One school visit I will always remember was my book talk of *Somewhere in the Darkness*. The class I met with was small, with students, mostly male, reading well below grade level. My standard talk was designed to end with a bit of a cliff-hanger, to encourage the students to read the book for themselves. However, once I introduced the story, the students in the class wanted to talk about Jimmy and his ex-con father, Crab.

They shared their own similar experiences, and the teacher later informed me that they insisted she read the book aloud to the entire class.

A visit from Walter Dean Myers provided something extra special for students. The Enoch Pratt Free Library was fortunate to host Walter on several occasions, mostly for well-attended public programs. For about six months, as he worked on *Malcolm X: By Any Means Necessary*, Walter visited two Baltimore middle schools monthly to talk about books, writing, and the importance of reading. This special project, coordinated by the Pratt Library and funded by the Margaret Alexander Edwards Trust, gave a lucky group of students unique insight into the working life of a writer. Walter shared research, revisions, and drafts of his manuscript, as well as his own thoughts on the life of the iconic Malcolm X. As I accompanied Walter on these visits, I observed firsthand his deep love for and commitment to young people.

Walter's work was always a great source for organized book discussions. When the Pratt Library began a family reading program in public housing, our first title was *Motown and Didi,* which led to a robust discussion about homelessness. *Monster* was the book of choice for one of our teen summer reading book clubs, and the young people even conducted their own mock trial. One of the liveliest gatherings was with middle-school book clubs from across Baltimore City meeting as "Freedom Readers," a joint project with the Greater Baltimore Urban League and the Pratt Library. One of the favorite book choices was *145th Street:*

Short Stories. Teens enjoyed the sense of community and the interconnectedness of everyone who lived on that block. The high caliber of the stories meant we were able to talk about characterization, tone, and the role of setting as well as the individual stories. Like so many of his titles, this collection hits all the right notes of humor, hardship, humanity, and hope, factors ever present in Walter's work and legacy.

Deborah Taylor recently retired from her role as coordinator of school and student services at the Enoch Pratt Free Library in Baltimore. She has chaired and served on many American Library Association committees, including those for the Robert F. Sibert Award, the Newbery Award, the Coretta Scott King Award, and the Printz Award. She was named the 2015 recipient of the Coretta Scott King–Virginia Hamilton Award for Lifetime Achievement. She is an adjunct professor of young adult literature at the University of Maryland, College of Information Studies.

LOIS LOWRY

Walter and I used to cross paths frequently at conventions and conferences. "Cross paths" is actually an inappropriate term, because if one encountered Walter on a path, there would be no way to get past him. He took up a lot of space! And, in any case, who would want to go past Walter? He always stopped with his (huge) smile to give a (huge) hug and to talk in his (huge) voice.

In 2003, he and I were among a group of authors who agreed to write short stories for an anthology that would be titled *Necessary Noise*. The editor, Michael Cart, had asked us to address the question, "What does 'family' mean today?" I wrote a story, "Snowbound," about a middle-class suburban family suffering through an excruciating weekend when their eighteen-year-old daughter brings a horrible boyfriend home from college. It had seven characters and took place over the course of two days.

Walter's story, "Visit," had two characters—a father and a son—and consisted of a conversation between them that lasted less than an hour.

My story was a forgettable chuckle. Walter's was a gut punch, and I'll remember it all my life.

He and I were the same age. Actually, that's a lie; we were born in the same year, but I was a few months older, and we joked about that now and then. I remember being astonished when I heard that he had died; there was a *no, that's impossible* feeling. He had seemed so alive, so timeless, and it was hard to conceive of such a vital personality being gone.

But he wasn't, really. He isn't. Some years have passed now, and we are still talking about him, still reading the words he wrote, still realizing the difference he made in so many lives.

Born in Hawaii in 1937, author Lois Lowry attended elementary school in Pennsylvania, junior high school in Tokyo, and high school in New York. She went to Brown University and the University of Southern Maine and holds honorary degrees from six universities. Currently, she divides her time between Maine and Florida.

Her close-to-fifty books for young people have been translated into twenty-seven languages, and two have been awarded the Newbery Medal. Several have been adapted for film and stage, and The Giver *has also been staged as an opera. Lowry is a mother of four and a grandmother of four, and has worked as a photojournalist and a writer of fiction. Lowry's newest book is* On the Horizon.

CLAUDETTE S. McLINN

I attended many of Walter Dean Myers's book signings and lectures, but the first time I really met him was in 1998 at the *Los Angeles Times* Festival of Books at UCLA. While I was working as the District Supervising Librarian in Media and Library Services for the Los Angeles Unified School District, my husband and I owned a children's bookstore in Inglewood. The bookstore was my calling. It was a labor of love, and only open on Saturdays (a long story).

We invited Walter to sign copies of his current book at our booth at the *Los Angeles Times* Festival of Books. He accepted, and we had a wonderful time. During this two-day weekend event, we were able to get to know him. He was passionate about encouraging African American boys to read, and made this offer: any African American boy who came into our bookstore could pick out a book and he (Walter) would pay for it. He himself had been a reluctant reader as a boy, he told us. Over the years, he intermittently sent grant monies to fulfill this personal mission.

The first work that I read by Walter was *Somewhere in the Darkness*, which was published in 1992. The story was compelling from the beginning to the end. I had not read anything like it. The book stayed with me and still stays with me. It is the story of Jimmy, a fourteen-year-old boy who lives with his grandmother while his father is in prison. His mother is deceased. One day, Jimmy comes home to find his grandmother out and a man named Crab there. Crab is Jimmy's father, and when his grandmother arrives home, Crab tells her that he wants to take Jimmy across the country. Then the adventure begins. This book won a Coretta Scott King Honor Award and a Newbery Honor. From then on, I read many of Walter's works.

The book that stands out most in my mind is the captivating and powerful *Monster,* which was published in 1999. This is a timeless work, relevant to today's issues of Black Lives Matter, the school-to-prison pipeline, and many social injustices. It's surprising that it has not yet been made into a movie. Through the years, I have book-talked *Monster* in our store and during presentations and have recommended it for book clubs. I am the cofounder of two book clubs, one for young people and one for adults; both clubs read the book and thoroughly enjoyed it. It elicited provocative discussions among all ages.

Walter's contribution to the field of children's literature is priceless. He wrote about African American subjects with honesty, realism, love, and pride. He knew the importance of writing culturally relevant books for children. He knew the importance of writing books as "mirrors" for children. In all honesty, Walter was a literary pioneer, making way for Jacqueline Woodson, Jason Reynolds, Kwame Alexander, and other well-known African American writers who address the Black experience. Walter's writing is relatable, and his legacy is secure. His books will stand the test of time.

Dr. Claudette S. McLinn is the executive director of the Center for the Study of Multicultural Children's Literature (CSMCL.org). She is the chair of the Coretta Scott King (CSK) Awards Committee and chair of the CSK 50th Anniversary Planning Committee. She has chaired and judged many other literary prizes, such as the Pura Belpré Medal, the Newbery Medal, the Caldecott Medal, the Ezra Jack Keats Award, the Kirkus Prize, and the Los Angeles Times *Book Prize in Young Adult Literature. Dr. McLinn is the recipient of numerous awards and honors, including the Dorothy McKenzie Award for Distinguished Contribution to the Field of Children's Literature, sponsored by the Children's Literature Council of Southern California.*

NATASHA DÍAZ

Before my mother and I moved to Harlem, we had been bouncing around for a while. My parents had separated four or five years prior, and my mother and I lived at my grandparents' house and then downtown in a basement apartment with rental code violations that became so infested with rats we had to leave in the middle of the night, multiple times. We were poor. We were doing our best. We were looking for a home. We found it in Harlem. Walter Dean Myers always wrote about Harlem in a way that held it up for its strength while not shying away from its struggles. He honored Harlem for what it is: a community and culture and neighborhood and people, a part of history often ignored or reduced to its faults. I hope Walter would see in this poem the Harlem we both love, the place we both found ourselves, and a peek into the spirit that makes Harlem feel so alive.

Sunday, September 16, 2001

Walter told us,
"Harlem was a promise." So, on Tuesday,
As tongues searched for hope between the gaps in gritted
    teeth,

That was what we tried to remember.

Silence rarely has a home up here
But we all heard the brownstones on 126th Street sigh,
Laden with despair,
Sturdy but tired,
Aged with dignity.
An army of distinguished brown strength.
The same type of lived-in and
Monuments to those years.
Shoulder to shoulder,
They hold each other up
As they held us down.

For six days,
Empty stoops sat shiva,
And Malcolm and Lenox bowed their heads on the corner
While our souls rattled between our ribs and fear,
As danger reported in color schemes and
We avoided the sky,
Trying to unsee the falling heartache debris.

Carrier pigeons woke us this morning.
They poked holes in the window screens to relay the
    message that
Nothing stops Sundays in Harlem.
Streets filled with songs and praise and church hats so tall
They bound the world we had been trapped in
To the one we pray to.

Teetering foot to foot on the line at Sylvia's,
Human dominoes lined up against each other,
Afraid to topple into questions.

What is the consequence for those who survived?
Will candied yams still taste sweet?

Relief swept us
As cavities danced across our mouths,
The flavor burrowed deep in our roots.

At some point,
I saw across the room,
Amidst the salve of laughter and gossip,
An old woman's wrinkles caressing her tears.

I don't know why she cried.
Maybe because this kind of familiar
Was only a mask
To the outside.

Or perhaps, in gratitude
That Harlem had kept its promise.

Natasha Díaz is a freelance writer and producer. As a screenwriter, Natasha has had scripts placed in the Austin Film Festival, the NALIP Diverse Women in Media Fellowship, and the Sundance Episodic Story Lab. Her personal essays have been published in The Establishment *and* HuffPost. *Her debut young adult novel is* Color Me In.

PAULETTA BROWN BRACY

How appropriate it is to celebrate Walter's legacy with the twentieth-anniversary reissue of *145th Street: Short Stories*. The collection of ten stories anchored in a close-knit community in his beloved Harlem explores the gamut of the human condition and its span of attendant emotions through first-person narratives of teenage residents. This work is an exquisite display of Walter's extraordinary skill in characterizing adolescence. Not only did he write for and about young adults, he wrote *to* them, addressing their issues in uncompromisingly realistic and authentic ways and with appropriate doses of empathy when needed. It was clear that he cared for his characters, and through the years, readers have comfortably connected with them.

I do not remember exactly when I met Walter. Over the course of the many years I participated in American Library Association and National Council of Teachers of English meetings, I attended sessions at which he appeared. I joined people standing patiently in long lines, awaiting the opportunity to be *up close and personal,* if only for a moment, with this rock star of the ages, as he signed our just-purchased books. He would greet each member of the fan club with a charming yet gentle smile that only heightened the thrill. Closing the book with the coveted signature, he would look up, smile again, and say, "Thank you." We thanked *him*. Again and again.

Today, we continue this tradition of immeasurable gratitude for Walter's outstanding body of work, most recently affirmed by the Children's Literature Legacy Award. In 1975, while working as a middle-school media specialist in a large urban district, I learned about an emerging African American male author of young adult literature. He had just published his first novel, *Fast Sam, Cool Clyde, and Stuff,* introducing readers to a colorful and endearing group of teens—three boys and a girl—living in Harlem and bonded in a special, abiding friendship. I was especially enthusiastic because I worked with male middle schoolers who had little interest in reading. From what I knew of this book, I saw potential for success! When I read it, I loved it and knew my students would want to read it. They responded favorably, intimately connecting with the characters who sounded like them and looked like them. In addition, the book created an interest in Harlem, which was little known among my students. This title was my first Walter Dean Myers experience and the beginning of long-term pure reading pleasure.

Walter published *Monster* in 1999. The story of Steve Harmon, a sixteen-year-old African American teen awaiting trial for murder, is told in complementary journal and screenplay formats. During his incarceration and trial, the protagonist reflects on his life, searching for his identity. The year before, I had been appointed to the Durham County Juvenile Crime Prevention Council (JCPC), which reviews the needs of juveniles who are at risk of delinquency or who have been adjudicated undisciplined or delinquent, and supports them with appropriate resources to address their needs. *Monster* became my favorite of all of Walter's works for two reasons. First, its timely intersection with my work on the council created a special relevance. Second, the masterful storyteller delivered a taut and riveting plot that hypnotically lured me into the jail cell, the courtroom, each journal entry, and each scene of the script. I was totally immersed in Steve Harmon's life. While reading the book, I also gained deeper insight into the *possible* psyche of incarcerated youth and how they might rationalize their dilemmas. Through this fine example of innovative writing, Walter broadened my understanding of the juvenile who regretfully becomes a part of the juvenile justice system.

I have discussed Walter's distinguished career as a writer, but I must also pay tribute to the other roles he played. I recognize him as a crusader for the cause who was dedicated to ensuring accurate representation of the African American experience for all readers. I knew him to be a mentor to many aspiring African American writers who have been fortunate beneficiaries of his wisdom, which he shared so generously. And I will always remember him as the voice for the village, bringing Harlem to life in his fiction, nonfiction, and poetry and celebrating its richness through every word.

Thank you, my most gifted griot.

Dr. Pauletta Brown Bracy is a professor at the School of Library and Information Sciences of North Carolina Central University, where she also serves as Director of the Office of University Accreditation. Her areas of teaching and research are school library media and children's and young adult literature and services with foci on ethnic perspectives in literature and meeting the needs of African American children and adolescents in school and public libraries. She is the 2019 recipient of the Coretta Scott King–Virginia Hamilton Award for Lifetime Achievement in the practitioner category. She holds a BA in English from Fisk University, an MLS from the University of Pittsburgh, and a PhD in library science from the University of Michigan.

CICELY LEWIS

Dear Walter Dean Myers,

Regrettably, your books were not in my school library, nor were they a part of the required reading list. I encountered your novels as a high school English teacher in Canton, Mississippi. I wanted a way to connect with my African American students and to teach them about their history. The novels in our bookroom were not connecting with them. They were tired of *To Kill a Mockingbird*. I found *The Glory Field* and I felt like I had discovered a secret treasure. Why wasn't this book on the required reading list? I put *Monster* in the hands of many students who believed reading was boring. I changed a few minds by doing this.

Fast-forward to 2017: I knew I had to do something different in my school. I was now the school librarian; therefore, every student in the building was my responsibility. There was a feeling of unrest in the air. Television screens and social media were constantly broadcasting stories of hate, fear, and violence against people who looked very much like my students and me. That is when I decided to create the Read Woke challenge.

What is Read Woke? It is a feeling. It is a style. It is a form of education. It is a call to action; it is our right as lifelong learners. It means arming yourself with knowledge in order to better protect your rights—

knowledge is power, and no one can take it away. It means learning about others so that you can treat people with the respect and dignity they deserve, no matter their race, creed, or color.

I decided that a Read Woke book must:

- *Challenge a social norm.*
- *Give voice to the voiceless.*
- *Provide information about a group that has been disenfranchised.*
- *Seek to challenge the status quo.*
- *Have a protagonist from an underrepresented or oppressed group.*

Students had to read books from the list and share their experiences. Upon doing so, they received a pin and a T-shirt.

You would be happy to know that the response has been amazing. Students are reading and becoming empowered to confront injustices across the world and in their communities. Just as you wished you had been introduced to *Sonny's Blues* by James Baldwin as a teen, I wish someone had introduced me to your work during my youth. Many times I felt alone, and I used books as my escape. It would have been nice to use books as a mirror. Because of this, I have it made it my life's mission to help provide students with books that provide a mirror for their own lives and a window into the lives of others. I want my students to become social justice warriors.

Before there was Read Woke, there was *Monster.* Before there was *Dear Martin, Long Way Down,* or *Ghost Boys,* there was *Scorpions.* I started the Read Woke challenge because my students, school, and community were hurting. Librarians around the world have taken up the charge and decided that their students deserve representation and exposure. Your work inspires not only writers but also children everywhere. I want my school library to be to my students what the George Bruce Branch of the New York Library on West 125th Street was to you: a haven.

When you interviewed a prosecutor who stated that his goal when representing his juvenile clients was to humanize them to the jurors, you realized that that was what you hoped to achieve with your books. That is also my goal as a teacher and a librarian—to humanize our experiences. I plan to carry on your legacy with Read Woke. Thank you for paving the way and writing woke.

Sincerely,
Cicely Lewis

Named a 2019 Library Journal Mover and Shaker, *Cicely Lewis is a school librarian with a passion for creating lovers of reading. In 2017, she started the Read Woke challenge in response to the shootings of young unarmed black boys, the repeal of DACA, and the lack of diversity in young adult literature. She inspired the nation to Read Woke, and educators across the world joined in and shared the movement with their students. A native of Mississippi, Cicely currently lives in Georgia with her husband, Michael, and their two children, Tristan and Trinity. When she is not reading, you can find Cicely writing her bimonthly column in* School Library Journal, *where she shares her book recommendations.*

RENÉE WATSON

Harlem is the incubator of dreams.

Harlem is the Black boy drumming on buckets in front of the Adam Clayton Powell statue on 125th Street, is the street vendor calling out what's for sale, is old-school hip-hop blaring from speakers, serenading tourists as they walk by wide-eyed and awestruck. Harlem is the woman at the window of a brownstone, watching and knowing all the comings and goings of the block; is the head nod, dap, fist pump, handshake, tight hug given to loved ones.

Harlem is always past, always present, always future, all at once.

Harlem is Countess Cullen, is James Baldwin, is Langston Hughes.

Harlem is Walter Dean Myers.

I fell in love with Harlem because of these writers. They loved Harlem in all its complexity and nuance, in all its glory and exquisiteness. This is to say, they loved Blackness, loved Black people. They wrote about Harlem, about Black boys and girls, with a fierce love.

And maybe this is one of the greatest takeaways from Walter's work. He did not write about what he did not love. There is always care, always grace on the page. No pity, no judgment.

Reading Walter's work is like taking a master class in writing. His work taught me how to care for my characters. How to make my stories about their humanity, not only their circumstances. He taught me how to love misunderstood places, how to look at a place from many angles, how to listen to its laughter, how to see its pain and struggle. How to recognize the different ways a community loves.

In Walter's stories, love is giving someone flowers while they are living and not waiting for a funeral to honor their life; it is the banter between friends debating who the greatest boxer is. Love is the look friends give each other, a knowing without having to say a word. Love tries to cheer up a friend who is down on himself for causing his team to lose the game.

Love shows up, always. It shows up in the darkest of moments. In "Big Joe's Funeral" and "The Baddest Dog in Harlem," there are devastating moments when the reader sees unfair, dehumanizing treatment of Black boys and men. There is a matter-of-fact way these scenes play out, showing how normalized and frequent these incidents are. Walter writes with great restraint, and at the moment when despair could settle in for both narrator and reader, he gives us a tender reminder that life is the good and the bad all at once. And this is another lesson I learned from Walter: the importance of giving hopeful, not necessarily happy, endings. In Walter's short stories he lets the reader know that the main character will be okay even if circumstances don't change, even if tomorrow there will be more heartache. Sometimes the happy ending is not complete resolution but a knowing that the characters we've grown to care about have each other, still. That even in this hard life—and maybe because of it—they still have love.

When I first moved to Harlem, my heart fluttered as I walked 145th Street. Walter's short stories came to life, and they remain accurate and relevant today. His Harlem is still vibrant, still complex, still alluring, still exemplifying that simple and profound love.

Renée Watson is a New York Times *bestselling author, educator, and activist. Her young adult novel,* Piecing Me Together, *received a Coretta Scott King Award and a Newbery Honor. Her children's picture books and novels for teens have received several awards and earned international recognition. Renée is the founder of I, Too Arts Collective, a literary-arts nonprofit housed in the Harlem brownstone where Langston Hughes lived and created.*

RUDINE SIMS BISHOP

I first "met" Walter Dean Myers on the day I defended my dissertation. A bit nervous still, but somewhat relieved, I returned to my graduate-student office after my defense and found on my desk a copy of his picture book *The Dragon Takes a Wife*. It provided just what I needed—a good laugh. A parody of a traditional fairy tale, it is the story of Harry, the lonely dragon who needs to defeat the knight in shining armor in order to win a wife. Harry keeps losing weekly bouts until he seeks help from the good-hearted but inept African American fairy Mabel Mae Jones. Mabel Mae greets Harry with "What's bugging you, baby?" and proceeds in her own hip way to try to help—unsuccessfully—until Harry suggests that she become a dragon to show him exactly how to move when he fights the knight. He falls in love with dragon Mabel Mae, they get married, he gets a good job in the post office, and they live happily ever after.

Myers went on to become one of the premier American writers of young adult fiction. We met in person a few years later when I was doing research for my first book on African American children's literature. I was looking for information on how the literature was developing. Walter agreed to an interview, and we met at a conference in San

Francisco to talk about issues in the field. His insights were very helpful in shaping my work.

Some time later, I was asked to write a biocritical work about Walter for the Twayne Young Adult Author Series (*Presenting Walter Dean Myers*, 1991). In my first book, I had identified Walter as an "image-maker," one of five African American writers whose work had shaped the early development of contemporary African American children's fiction. Research for this project called for a visit to his New Jersey home, where I met his gracious wife, Constance, and their charming and gifted then-teenage son, Christopher.

One of the things that became clear about Walter was that he deeply cared about young people. We visited a group of middle-school writers he was mentoring at the time, and I was able to observe how gentle he was in his criticism even while insisting that they put in the effort to improve their writing. This affection for young people comes through in his talk about his work and in his books, especially those that portray and celebrate what he called "vertical living," life among teenage African American boys in urban settings.

Myers was born in West Virginia, but he grew up in Harlem, and that setting is prominent in his early books. He had an unerring ear for the rhetoric of young African American men—at least those living in the late twentieth century—as well as a deep appreciation for the problems they face, and insights into their strengths and their abilities to solve those problems. He also offered much-needed humor and a sense of hope.

Although he is best known for his urban fiction, Myers was willing to tackle various genres. In addition to his young adult fiction, he produced histories, biographies, short stories, poetry (including rhymes for young children), and picture books, all of which were critically well received. He wrote over a hundred books all together.

Walter once noted that he was inspired by Langston Hughes and James Baldwin, whose works demonstrated that his own neighborhood and its inhabitants were rich sources of stories. The stories in *145th Street* exemplify Walter's skill at capturing and representing the lives of African American teens and adults in one urban community. He takes the reader to Harlem and offers vivid portraits of characters who live on the block, celebrating the lives of these ordinary people. He asserted that he wanted "to tell Black children about their humanity and about their history and how to grease their legs so the ash won't show and how to braid their hair so it's easy to comb on frosty winter mornings." He and his wisdom are sorely missed, and I, for one, am glad to see this gem of a book reissued on its twentieth anniversary.

Dr. Rudine Sims Bishop is professor emerita of education at the Ohio State University, where she has taught courses on children's literature. Her books include Shadow *and* Substance: Afro-American Experience in Contemporary Children's Fiction; Presenting Walter Dean Myers; Kaleidoscope: A Multicultural Booklist for Grades K–8; *and* Wonders: The Best Children's Poems of Effie Lee Newsome. *She has won several awards and has been on the selection committees for both the Caldecott and Newbery Medals.*

JASON REYNOLDS

Walter Dean Myers and Jason Reynolds walk into a school.

This could be the setup for a funny joke.

This would also be, for me, a dream come true.

Walter and I, two too-tall men, scribbling our names in the ledger in the main office. IDs checked, scanned. Stickers printed, slapped on our chests. Visitors. Walter complains about the sticker but stops once the librarian arrives to walk us down to the auditorium for sound check.

"Jason, just tell me what you had for breakfast," the sound man says.

"Black coffee, two bananas."

"And you, Walter?"

Walter says something about how he's eaten French toast. Or pancakes. Or both. And a steak. And a gallon of ice cream. And a head of lettuce. But he hasn't had any of this. He just thinks it's funny, especially since the young people have started to file in and can hear him.

They line the rows, sitting side by side, some slapping their neighbors' arms. Some slumping down in their seats, hoods pulled over their heads. Some straight-backed, attentively waiting. And Walter and I lean against the stage and watch how all of them, at some point—for unknown reasons—throw their bodies into dance. Sometimes just a single move; other times a combination of moves. Juts and jukes. Mostly hands doing all the work, a spastic symphonic sign language.

Walter leans over. He says, "This . . . is different."

I nod. "Yeah, they dance all the time now, even when there's no music."

"Or maybe there is music, Jason," Walter says, flashing a smile. "A jazz, a funk, a bop only they can hear."

"Maybe," I say with a shrug. And Walter, with one arm over my shoulder and the other peeling the visitor sticker from his chest, just nods knowingly.

Jason Reynolds is a New York Times *bestselling author, a Newbery Award honoree, a Printz Award honoree, a National Book Award honoree, a Kirkus Prize winner, a two-time Walter Dean Myers Award winner, an NAACP Image Award winner, and the recipient of multiple Coretta Scott King Honors. The American Booksellers Association's 2017 and 2018 spokesperson for Indies First, his many books include* When I Was the Greatest, Boy in the Black Suit, All American Boys *(cowritten with Brendan Kiely),* As Brave as You, For Every One, *the Track series (*Ghost, Patina, Sunny, *and* Lu*), and* Long Way Down, *which received both a Newbery Honor and a Printz Honor. He lives in Washington, DC.*

NIC STONE

Monster was first. And I'd never read anything like it.

It cracked my world open in more ways than I could count. I was blown away by the format and riveted by the plot, yes. But also, it's a book that says so much about the inner lives of kids who get arrested. The lives we fail to see once the kids are in those orange jumpsuits. Steve got caught up in some foolishness, yes. But he also had big dreams, and the talent to make them come true.

Then *Darius & Twig*. A book about the Struggle, yes. But also about the power of friendship and the importance of mutual edification and HOPE. Holding one another down.

There was *Lockdown*, which provided a stunning window into the life of a kid who really just wants out of jail, but can't seem—for reasons that made perfect sense—to stop getting into the kind of trouble that will keep him there. *Street Love*, one of the first books in verse I ever read, and one that gender-flipped the good-girl/bad-boy trope in a way I haven't seen before or since. *All the Right Stuff*, which explains the concept of the social contract using examples young black people can relate to. *Dope Sick*, a book just as relevant now as when it was first published a decade ago.

And then there was *Shooter*. The book that made it all click. The book that made me realize that the magic of

Walter Dean Myers lay not only in the stories he pulled into the spotlight, but in the way he angled the spotlight. The transcripts used in this book—conversations between an investigator and kids connected to a school shooting—made me realize that the method employed in telling a story is just as important as the story itself.

Form.

And it forever changed both the stories *I* want to tell and the way that I want to tell them.

I never had the privilege of meeting Mr. Myers, but it's safe to say that everything I write is, in a way, a tribute to him and his vast body of work.

145th Street, a YA collection of connected short stories that gives a paradigm-shifting glimpse at a slice of American life that is often not only misrepresented but also caricaturized in a way that perpetuates dangerous—and false—stereotypes. A book cut into ten bits that give the effect of shifting a single diamond so that a beam of light refracts off its facets.

It's magic.

And so was he.

Nic Stone is an Atlanta native and a Spelman College graduate. After working extensively in teen mentoring and living in Israel for several years, she returned to the United States to write full-time. Nic's debut novel for young adults, Dear Martin, *was a New York Times bestseller and William C. Morris Award finalist. She is also the author of* Odd One Out, *a novel about discovering oneself and who it is okay to love, which was an NPR Best Book of the Year and a Rainbow Book List Top Ten selection, and* Jackpot, *a love-ish story that takes a searing look at economic inequality.*

HARLEM: THEN AND NOW

HARLEM'S BEGINNINGS

Harlem is a district in the northern section of New York City's Manhattan borough. Although it does not have fixed boundaries, most people agree that the neighborhood begins at 96th Street (east of Central Park) and 110th Street and Cathedral Parkway (north and west of Central Park) and ends at 155th Street to the north. The eastern boundaries are the East and Harlem rivers, and the western boundary is Amsterdam Avenue. In addition to the modern vibrant culture, the area has a rich past with roots that extend back for centuries.

Harlem was first settled by the Wecksquaesgeek Native American tribe. In 1639, the Dutch settled in the area, renaming it Nieuw Haarlem (New Harlem) after a city in Holland. In 1664, the British invaded and later simplified the name to Harlem. The area was a battleground during the Revolutionary War, most famously during the Battle of Harlem Heights in 1776.

THE RISE OF INDUSTRIALIZATION

Until the 1880s, Harlem consisted primarily of undeveloped land and farmland. But as Manhattan became increasingly populated, industrialization soared. Construction on the Harlem Railroad began in the 1830s and initiated a real estate boom. Developers jumped on the opportunity to build brownstones and apartments for wealthy white families, but when the boom ended, they found themselves with more vacant apartments than potential tenants. By the 1870s, the New York Elevated Railway company inexpensively linked downtown and uptown New York City by train. Soon, Jewish, Italian, and West Indian immigrant families from the Lower East Side flocked to this less populated section of town and diversified the neighborhood.

In the early 1900s, the excess of housing in Harlem resulted in a real estate crash that left many landlords desperate to fill their properties. At the time, many real estate agents in Harlem would only rent to white tenants. However, Philip Payton, a Black man working as a barber, a handyman, and a porter at a real estate office, seized an opportunity and began managing properties for white agents. He rented these properties to Black Americans, simultaneously acquiring his own buildings. Eventually, Payton created the Afro-American Realty Company, a business that bought and rented properties solely for Black tenants. Because of Payton's realty business, the Black population across Northern Manhattan greatly increased.

A few years after the founding of the Afro-American Realty Company, even greater changes began to occur across the country. In a post–Civil War United States, Black codes (unjust labor laws for Black citizens, specifically in Southern states), Jim Crow laws (state and local regulations that enforced racial segregation), sharecropping practices, and white supremacist organizations such as the Ku Klux Klan disenfranchised Black people and posed daily dangers in Southern states. During this period, starting in 1916, many Black Americans left the South and relocated to the industrialized North, Midwest, and West, seeking social and financial opportunity in cities like New York, Chicago, and Detroit. Over several decades, more than six million Black Americans took part in what became known as the Great Migration.

THE HARLEM RENAISSANCE

The influx of Black Americans into Manhattan contributed to the Harlem Renaissance, a period of cultural and artistic expression that began in the late 1910s and lasted about twenty years. During this time, Black artists, intellectuals, and activists sought to break free from white stereotypes of Black Americans and Black culture. Although this cultural explosion was not limited solely to New York City, many iconic leaders and landmarks emerged from Harlem's bustling neighborhood.

Philosopher, writer, and educator Alain Locke is often considered the Father of the Harlem Renaissance for publishing *The New Negro*, an anthology of fiction, essays, poetry, drama, music, and visual art. W. E. B. Du Bois, scholar and civil rights leader, cofounded the National Association for the Advancement of Colored People (NAACP) in 1909 and contributed to the discourse surrounding race, society, and civil rights in the organization's official magazine, *The Crisis*. Celebrated poet Langston Hughes and renowned author Zora Neale Hurston were activists who used their work to provoke critical thought and advocate for change. Performers including Louis Armstrong, Duke Ellington, Dizzy

Gillespie, Ella Fitzgerald, Billie Holiday, Bessie Smith, and others took part in the movement through their contributions to jazz and blues music. Other entertainers, such as dancer and singer Josephine Baker and actor Paul Robeson, enjoyed great success. Additionally, the visual arts world was transformed by the unique techniques and talents of artists such as Aaron Douglas and Palmer Hayden. These prominent figures represent only a small number of the prolific creators of the time, members of Harlem's vibrant community who made a lasting impact on American culture.

MIDCENTURY ACTIVISM AND BEYOND

The Great Depression hit in 1929, during the later years of the Harlem Renaissance. Lasting until 1939, the Great Depression was a period of economic struggle that spawned financial difficulties across the globe. In the United States, these stressors—in combination with widespread racism—led to increased social mobilization and activism in Black communities. Tensions reached a fever pitch in 1964 during the Harlem Race Riot. When James Powell, a fifteen-year-old Black teenager, was shot by a white off-duty police officer, many Harlem residents were infuriated and took to the streets to peacefully protest. Protests continued, and during a march to the Harlem police station two days later, the demonstrations became violent and spread from Manhattan to Brooklyn and Queens. The riot lasted six days, killing one and injuring more than one hundred people.

However, the Harlem Race Riot was a reaction to only

one of the many injustices felt around the country. From the mid 1950s through the late 1960s, the civil rights movement spread across the United States. Activists demanded equal rights and treatment for Black Americans. During this time, Harlem was often a planning ground that fostered iconic leaders. Malcolm X championed rights for Black Americans, and Adam Clayton Powell Jr. became the first Black person from New York elected to the US House of Representatives. As the movement continued to grow, organizations such as the Black Panther Party formed new chapters nationwide, including in Harlem. These efforts, in Harlem and around the country, led to policies that enforced racial equality regarding education, housing, marriage, employment, voting rights, and many other aspects of daily life.

HARLEM TODAY

Today, the power and beauty of Harlem shines in the iconic structures and areas that remain in this vibrant neighborhood. Local community organizations are actively maintaining the history and culture of the area for both longtime residents and visitors from around the globe. From lush parks to museums to places of worship, the following list offers a quick snapshot of modern Harlem.

MUSIC, THEATER, AND ART

- **Minton's Playhouse** is an iconic jazz club that is recognized for its role in the conception of modern jazz music. Saxophonist Henry Minton founded the club in 1938 and attracted talented performers such as Dizzy Gillespie, Thelonius Monk, Miles Davis, Charlie Parker, and Count Basie. The still-active club, located on 118th Street, is part of the US National Register of Historic Places.

- **The Apollo Theater**, located on 125th Street, is a historic music hall known for featuring African American performers. It opened in 1914 as Hurtig & Seamon's New Burlesque Theater and initially permitted only white customers. However, after a temporary close, the establishment reopened in 1934 as the integrated Apollo Theater. A host of classic and modern stars have performed at the Apollo, from Billie Holiday to Marvin Gaye to Lauryn Hill.

- **The Studio Museum**, located on 127th Street, is devoted to art and artists of African descent. The gallery opened in 1968 and features pieces ranging from drawings to photographs to mixed-media installations. The collection includes art from famed creators such as painter Jacob Lawrence, mixed-media and interdisciplinary artists Romare Bearden and Terry Adkins, graphic artist and sculptor Elizabeth Catlett, and many more.

- **The Schomburg Center for Research in Black Culture** is a research library within the New York Public Library system. The center holds artifacts and resources related to the experiences and history of individuals of African descent. The library was established in 1925 using founder

Arturo Alfonso Schomburg's collection of books, manuscripts, paintings, and other historical material. Located on Malcolm X Boulevard, it is a National Historic Landmark, and its collection boasts more than 11 million items.

PLACES OF WORSHIP

- **Abyssinian Baptist Church** was founded in 1808 by African American women and men who rejected the segregated seating at their previous church, First Baptist Church of New York City. The church was given Ethiopia's ancient name, Abyssinia, and became the first African American Baptist church in New York state. The religious organization supported the Harlem community over the decades by aiding residents during the Great Depression and promoting civil rights activism. In 1993, Abyssinian Baptist Church was named an official city landmark. The structure is located on 138th Street.

- Formed in 1796, **Mother African Methodist Episcopal (AME) Zion Church** is the oldest African American church in New York state. Like the founders of the Abyssinian Baptist Church, the founders of Mother AME Zion Church formed their own place of worship in response to the segregation within Methodist institutions. This church played a crucial role in history as a stop on the Underground Railroad and was known as the "Freedom Church." Located on 137th Street, the institution is known for its activism-focused services and has drawn celebrities such as W. E. B. Du Bois, Langston Hughes, Madam C. J. Walker, and Paul Robeson.

- **Masjid Malcolm Shabazz Mosque,** originally known as The Nation of Islam's Temple No. 7 (or Muhammad's Temple of Islam #7), was originally founded in 1956 by Elijah Muhammad and El Hajj Malik Shabazz (the civil rights activist also known as Malcolm X). In 1965, shortly after Malcolm X's assassination, the building was firebombed. However, the structure was rebuilt and renamed Masjid Malcolm Shabazz Mosque in 1975. Today, the place of worship is located on 116th Street.

HISTORIC BUILDINGS

- The **Hamilton Grange National Memorial** is the preserved home of Founding Father Alexander Hamilton. The home was originally completed in 1802 and was relocated twice in Harlem—in 1889 to Convent Avenue, in 2006 to St. Nicholas Park. The surrounding neighborhood was named Hamilton Heights after this thirty-two-acre estate, and the memorial has been listed on the National Register of Historic Places since 1966.

- The **Corn Exchange Building,** also known as Mount Morris Bank Building, was erected in 1880. The building not only was the home of the Mount Morris Bank (later known as the Corn Exchange Bank) but also held both residential and commercial spaces. It is cherished for its unique architecture and was added to the National Register of Historic Places in 1989. After a terrible fire in 1997, the building was renovated and reopened to the public as an office and retail space.

- The **369th Regiment Armory** is an arsenal constructed in 1913 that supported the African American National Guard soldiers of World War I. This regiment of Black soldiers was also known as the Harlem Hellfighters, and they spent more time in combat than any other similarly sized American unit. This Art Deco armory was added to the National Register of Historic Places in 1994.

PARKS AND GREEN SPACES

Harlem is home to a wealth of outdoor areas where residents host barbecues, parties, and community events. **Marcus Garvey Park,** originally known as Mount Morris Park, was opened in 1840. The park was renamed in 1973 for Marcus Garvey, an activist and advocate for economic independence within the Black community. **Jackie Robinson Park** was originally established as Colonial Park in 1911. However, it was renamed in 1978 in honor of Robinson, the first Black baseball player in the major leagues. Other historic parks include **St. Nicholas Park** and **Morningside Park** (both created in 1895). Today, local preservation organizations seek to keep these parks clean, well maintained, and available to the public for programming and recreation.